Kapalkundala

Kapalkundala

Bankim Chandra Chatterjee

MINT EDITIONS

Kapalkundala was first published in 1885.

This edition published by Mint Editions 2021.

ISBN 9781513299372 | E-ISBN 9781513224039

Published by Mint Editions®

 **MINT
EDITIONS**

minteditionbooks.com

Publishing Director: Jennifer Newens
Design & Production: Rachel Lopez Metzger
Project Manager: Micaela Clark
Translated by Devendra Nath Ghose
Typesetting: Westchester Publishing Services

Contents

Foreword

Kapalkundala is unquestionably one of many masterpieces of Bankim Chandrand this fact, I think, will be deemed a sufficient apology for bringing it out in an English garb. Besides the style, perhaps the most perfect in our language, the masterly delineation of human character and sentiment, the beauty of its descriptive passages, the high imaginative colouring and the sombre background lend to this romance a singular place among the fictions of Bengal, if not, of the world. Such a work should be the common property of man. It is, indeed, impossible to transfer the graces of style and diction from one language to another as much of the spirit is lost with the translation. However, the task here imposed upon the translator has been to convey, through the medium of the most wide-spread language in the world, something of the beauties of the original work. The main charm centres in the character of Kapalkundala around whom the whole plot gravitates. Such a character is unique in its creation, perhaps, unparalleled in any literature. She was indeed, a child of nature, as Miranda or Sakuntala was, though she was something different from either. Miranda and Sakuntala knew the ways of the world but she was naturally ignorant of them. The warm passion of love was singularly wanting in her. When she met Nabokumar she felt for him not what Miranda felt for Fardinand or Sakuntala for Dussanto but she felt for him what a kind-hearted woman feels for a benighted traveller. Even her married life brought no change. Nature gave her the best education—the endless sea, the vast sky, the broad and general air enlarged her heart. She was all sacrifice without the faintest tinge of selfishness in her. The only human training she received that imparted by the Kapalik and Adhicary and that was complete self-abnegation. Such a flower will grow best by the sea-side in the open air and sunshine. It must wither when transplanted to the flower pot of the hot-house of an artificial society with all its formalities and hypocrisies, and so the story ended in a tragedy. The translator is aware of the many imperfections in his work and as it has been hurried through the press, he craves the indulgence of his readers, for any errors that might have crept into it.

CALCUTTA. 18th August, 1919
Charu Chandra Palit

PART I

I

At the Estuary of the Ganges

Nearly two hundred and fifty years have passed away since the grey hours of one Magh morning saw a passenger-boat making her way up the river on her voyage back from the Saugor Islands. It was usual at that time for such boats to sail in strong parties on account of the scare of the Portuguese and other pirates. But these passengers had no companion-boats. The reason was that a thick fog had overspread the horizon towards the latter part of the night. The crew, having lost their bearings, drifted a far long way from the little flotilla. Now there was no knowing which direction she was making for. Most of the people on board were asleep. Only an old man and a youth lay awake, the former conversing with the latter. The former for a moment broke off and addressed one of the crew: "Boatman, what distance can you cover this day?"

"I can hardly say" replied the boatman after a short indecision.

The interrogator took offence and began railing at the boatman. "What is in the hands of Providence, Sir" chipped in the youth, "can't be foretold by the wise, far less by a simpleton. You must not bother over that."

"Not bother!" echoed back the other furiously. "What do you mean? The fellows forcibly cut away paddy from some twenty odd bighas of my land and what my children would live upon the whole year?"

This news he received from the fresh arrivals not before he had come out to the Saugor Islands. "So I observed already" rejoined the youngman, "when you have none other guardian left home, it was wrong of you to venture out."

"Not venture!" snapped the old man as sharply as before. "Three quarters of my life have been spent and only the fourth is left. Now or never to work for one's next life."

"If I have read the scriptures aright," added the youth, "the merits of pilgrimages accruing to after-life are equally within the reach of those who stay at home."

"Why did you stir out then?" returned the old man. "So I told you at the very outset," replied the other, "I had a great mind to have a look at the sea. So I came." Then he exulted half to himself "Ah! what a sight! This is never to be forgotten in ages of the soul's migrations."

> *"From afar, as on a wheel of iron, slender*
> *All blue with tamarisks and palms extended,*
> *Outshines the briny oceans' margin yonder,*
> *Like streak of rust-mark with the wheel-rim blended."*

The elderly man's ear was not following the poetry but he was listening raptly to the conversation passing among the crew.

"Eh, brother, our folly is looking the bigger" spoke one of the crew to the other. "Are we out on the open sea now, or in what corner of the globe the boat has got to, can't understand." The speakers voice had the ring of a great fright. The old man scented some danger ahead and nervously enquired "Boatman, is anything the matter?" The man addresssed to did not answer. But the young blood waited not for the reply. He came out into the bare open and saw the day was dawning. The heavy pall of a thick mist lay over everything. The stars, the moon, the sky, the coast-line were all blotted out. He understood that the crew had lost all directions. They were not certain which way they were steering the boat. They feared they would perish in the boundless open sea.

A screen hung out in front as cold protector and the passengers were quite in the dark about all this. But the young man knew the plight and explained to the old man the whole thing in detail. Then arose a great uproar aboard. Of the female passengers some awoke at the sound of the conversation and no sooner had their ears caught the remark than they set up a loud wail. "Row shoreward, row shoreward, row shoreward," vociferated the elderly man.

The youth smiled softly and put in "where is the shore? If we could but know this, how would the danger arise?"

Now louder grew the hub-bub. The youth quieted them down somehow and said "Have no fear. The day has broken and the sun rises within two odd hours. The boat can never sink by that period. Now stop rowing and let her go adrift. Next when the sun breaks through, we would lay our heads together."

The crew approved of this bit of advice and acted accordingly.

All boathands sat stockstill. The passengers ate their hearts out in an agony of suspense. The wind blew a gentle sigh. The shake of the boat was scarcely felt on account of the smooth glassy sea. However, they felt sure that their last hour had struck. Silently did men say their prayers and loudly did women raise a babel of cries uttered in vocal contortions of different keys. One of them had given a watery grave to her babe in the deep water of the Bay—she had dropped her child but could not rescue it—she of all others did not weep.

While in this nervous mood of expectancy, they guessed it to be nine o'clock. At that time the crew all on a sudden shouted out at the top of their lungs the names of the five Pirs of water and kicked up a row. All on board burst in one voice "What, what is up?" All the boathands cried out in a chorus. "The sun has appeared. Land ahoy." Every body crawled out into the open space and began to observe the locality and the surroundings. They saw the sun had come out and the mist rolled away like a curtain before the sun revealing all sides in their naked clearness. The sun shone pretty above the horizon line. The water on which the boat floated was not the sea but the estuary of a river though the same expanse was scarcely observable any where else. One side of the river was within easy reach—it was twenty-five yards more or less from where the boat lay. But the coast-line was hardly visible on the opposite side. Every other way besides, shimmered the wild waste of water in the glare of the brilliant sun and sweeping off immeasurably melted into the misty sky-line. The adjacent water had a turbid appearance as is usually noticeable in river water though the same looked blue at a distance. They felt certain that they had drifted down into the deep blue sea. But by some stroke of good luck they were pretty near the land. So they screwed up some courage. They calculated the direction from the sun's position. The fringe of the frontal ground was easily concluded to be the western seaboard. At a close range from where the boat floated was the mouth of another river pouring its gurgling flow of gold into the channel. Innumerable water-birds of diverse description were playing joyously on the broad patch of sand that lay on the southern side of the estuary. This stream now takes the name of the Rasulpur river.

II

ON THE COAST

The first impulses of elation being over, the crew proposed that as there was still time for the tide to come, the passengers in the meantime might cook and dine on the sands before them and with the rising tide might start on the way home. The men fell in with the suggestion. Then the boatmen having secured the boat along the bank, the men landed. They had had their dips in the water before they attended to their morning ceremonies.

After bath before starting kitchen-work another difficulty presented itself in the shape of the absence of any fuel on board. Every one was loth to fetch firewood from the high bank on account of tigerscare. At last the dread of sheer starvation staring them in the face, the old man proposed to the previously mentioned youth "Nabokumar, my boy, we so many people would die, if you can not cast about for any means."

Nabokumar reflected a few seconds and replied "All right, I shall go. Let a man bear me company with a wood-cutting knife and an axe."

No body, however, responded to the call.

With the words "The affair would be squared up at the meal-time," Nabokumar girded up his loins and axe in hand, set out in search of fuel.

When Nabokumar ascended the higher ridges of the river slope, his wandering eye could not see any vestige of human habitation within the whole stretch of ground. It was but a weald, though the wood consisted neither of stately trees nor dense brushwood. Only at intervals, shrubs grew up in circular forms and covered the ground. As Nabokumar could not find there any firewood proper to fell, he wandered on to the remoter reaches of the upland in quest of any suited to his purpose. At last he found out a fellable tree and provided himself with the necessary fuel. The transport of the load seemed another uphill task. Nabokumar was not born of a poor parentage. So he was not inured to such hard jobs. Besides, he had not considered the question in all its bearings before he started on his mission. Now the carrying of the wood proved a sharp work. However Nabokumar was not a man to shirk a task to which he had set his hand because of its arduous nature. Therefore, he trudged along with the bundle over a certain distance and when he grew tired, he rested at stages and again proceeded. He plodded his way back in this way.

This delayed Nabukumars' return. On the other hand his companions felt nervous as there had been none of the noticeable signs of his return. They feared Nabokumar had been killed by a tiger. The allowable time-limit being over, they came to that positive conclusion. Still no body ventured to go up the bank and advance a few paces in search of Nabokumar.

The passengers were indulging in such idle thoughts when the terrible moan of rushing tide was audible in the water. The crew fully knew it to be the on-rush of the coming tide. Besides, they knew that with the flood-tide, the heaving water dashed against the coastline with such a fury that any boat happening to lie on the coastal water was sure to be smashed to smithereens. So with great bustle they unfastened the mooring and made for the midstream. No sooner was the boat untied than the river-fringe was flooded over. The passengers could scarcely find time to spring on to the boat's side when the rice and grain deposited on the margin were clean washed-away. To add to their misfortunes, the crew were not skilled boatmen. They could not steady the boat. So the boat was pitched into the Rasulpur river-channel with the violence of the current. One of the passengers cried "Nabokumar is left behind." One of the crow replied "Alas! Is your Nabokumar alive? He is safe in the stomach of a jackal."

So the boat was being rushed up the Rasulpur river by the rapid current. But as it would be an arduous task to get the boat downstream afterwards, the crew were trying their level best to emerge from the river. Even in that cold month of Magh sweat started out and trickled down their brows. Though they forced their way back from the river-channel with such exertion, yet no sooner did the boat come out than she was caught up by the more violent stream outside. The boat shot up due north like an arrow and the crew could not bring themselves to control her. The boat never returned.

By the time the current slackened down so as to let the boat being tackled, the passengers were carried over a long distance past the mouth of the Rasulpur river. Now the question whether they would retrace their course furnished food for discussion. We ought to say here that Nabokumars' fellow-passengers were all his neighbours but none his kinsmen. They concluded that they would have to await another low-tide to come back. Then night would fall when further navigation would be impossible and they would have to wait for another hightide. This meant starvation for each and all throughout the period. Thus two days' privations would bring them within an ace of death. The more so, when the crew remained obdurate and would obey no orders. They asserted that Nabokumar had been killed by a tiger. This was possible. If so, then what would all their worries avail?

Concluding thus, the people thought it judicious to get back homeward without Nabokumar. Nabokumar was thus left to his fate in the howling sea-side wilderness.

If at this, any body sets his face against be-stirring himself in search of fire-wood to save others from starvation, he deserves the world's ridicule. Let those people whose nature it is to send out their benefactors into exile ply their "dirty work" an the while; but men who run about to collect fire-wood for others must do the same, over and again, whatsoevertimes they are banished from their hearth-stone. Because you are bad makes for no reason why I should not be good.

III

IN SOLITUDE

Not far off from the place where Nabokumar was cast away, now stand two straggling villages under the names of Daulatpur and Dariapur. But at that period of which we are speaking, there could scarcely be visible any signs of human habitation. It was all woodland. The part of this countryside was not so as other parts of Bengal which are usually flat. An unbroken range of sand-dunes traversed the whole stretch of ground lying between the mouth of the Rasulpur river and the Subarnarekha. If the series of the sand-elevations would have been a little bigger in height, these might have claimed the appellation of a chain of sandhills. Now people call these the Baliari. The white cliffs of the Baliari or sandhills appear unusually bright under the hot meridian sun. No tall trees grow on those heights. Shrubs and undergrowths abound at the feet of these sand-mounds though the arid desolate belt and summit generally emit a white glow. Of the plants overgrowing the downward slope, there is plenty of waterside shrubs comprising bushes and flowering creepers.

At such an unpleasant spot was Nabokumar abandoned by his companions. The first thing that struck his eye, on return to the riverside with the load of wood, was the absence of the boat at the water edge. Though a sudden great fear immediately sent a shiver into his heart, it looked next to impossible that he could be ever forsaken there by his fellow-travellers. An impression gained upon him that due to the swamping of the down by the hightide they might have taken the boat to some secure place and so they would find him out in no time. Fed by this hope, he sat down and lay in wait for some time. But neither the boat came nor did the men put in their appearance. Nobokamar's little mary craved for food and drink. Unable to wait any longer, he wandered over the river-fringe hunting for the boat. But the boat could not be found any where. So the retraced his steps and came back to the starting ground. Though till then he could not see the boat he laboured under the delusion that the boat might have been carried away by the tide-stream and so they would be late in getting back against current. Even when the tide ebbed he thought the boat could not return owing to violence of the stream against which she could hardly make any headway. Now she might come back as the tide was out. But now the ebb-tide settled into a slacker stream, the day declined and the sun went down. The boat would have returned by this time if she had been put back on the reverse course.

Then he concluded either the boat was wrecked by the violence of the tidal water or he was left to his fate in this lonely place by his fellow-passengers.

Nobokumar saw no village there—the place without shelter, without men, without food, without drink. The river water tasted bitter brine and his heart was being rent under the agony of hunger and thirst. He found not the shelter that could save him from the biting cold nor had he sufficient clothing on. He had the gloomy prospect of lying down for the night on the icy-cold-wind-swept river bank under the canopy of the unkind sky, unsheltered and unprotected. During night there was the chance of his meeting tigers and bears. In any case death was certain.

Owing to the restlessness of mind Nabokumar could not sit still on one spot for a considerable time. He left the fore-shore, clambered up and wandered aimlessly. Gradually the colour faded out from the sky and darkness fell. The stars came out in the frosty sky overhead as silently as they used to do in his native clime. Now this wooded country-side was hushed in darkness—the sky, the field, the sea were all bathed in a stillness punctuated with the dull continuous roar of the sea and the occasional howling of wild beasts rising above all this. Still in that darkness did Nabokumar tramp around these sand-dunes under the bleak sky. Up hill and down dale, now at the foot of the sandhills and then on their crests did he ramble about ceaselessly. At every step of this aimless ramble had he the chance of an attack from the wild beasts. But he had the same fear even when he placed himself on one spot. Nabokumar grew footsore and fatigued with such wandering. He had been fasting all day and so he became all the more weary. He sat down at a certain place supporting his back against a sand-mound and remembered his cosy bed at home. When a man broods in an exhausted condition of his mind and body, sleep sometimes steals a march and closes his drooping eyelids. Thus Nabokumar blooded and glided into a vague sort of forgetfulness. Perhaps, had this not been the order of things, then men in all ages could ill-stand the stress and strain of domestic troubles.

IV

On the top of a sand-hill

It was deep into night when Nabokumar awoke. He wondered that till then he was not killed by a tiger. He gave all sides his searching-glances, to be sure whether a tiger was stalking him or not. Suddenly he espied before him the glimmer of a light at a long distance. To guard against delusion, he strained his eyes after it. The orb of light grew by degrees in magnitude and brightness and he concluded it to be a fire-light. No sooner did Nabokumar conclude this, than his hope of life revived. No such light was possible without man because it was not the season of forest-fire. Nobokumar started to his feet. He ran towards the direction of the light. Once he thought "Is the glow of light a will-o'-the-wisp?—It might be so. But what life is saved if anybody lacks courage to confront the danger?" Prey to such thoughts, he moved forward with a brave heart aiming at the light. Trees, creepers and sandheaps obstructed him at every step. He trampled under feet plants and trailers, crossed over sand-dunes and walked onward. When he drew near the light, he saw a fire burning at the pretty altitude of a small sand-elevation and the picture of a man sitting on the top silhouetted against the sky-line in the glow. Resolved to approach the man seated on the hill-crest, Nabokumar pressed on with unslackened pace. At last he began to ascend the sand hill. Then he felt a bit nervous. However, he went on through the work with unshaken limbs. On nearing the man squatted there, his flesh creeped at what his eyes met with. He was indecisive whether to advance or withdraw.

The man seated on the height was absorbed in meditation with closed eyes. So he could not observe Nabokumar at first. Nabokumar saw the man on the verge of fifty. He could not perceive whether the man had any cloth on or not. He had a tiger-skin wrapped round his loins that reached to his knee and a string of Rudrakha round his neck. His big broad face was overgrown with shaggy hair and surmounted with a crown of matted locks.

A fire glowed before him—the same that acted the lodestar to Nabokumar to guide his steps there. An offensive smell stinked into his nostrils and he made out the reason when he happened to glance at the mans' seat. The man of matted locks sat on a headless corpse in a state of disintegration. He grew all the more alarmed when he detected a skull lying before him with some crimson liquid in the hollow. Around him were strewn about here and there bones whitened in the sand. Even the string of Rudrakha suspended round his neck had small bones fastened between them at intervals. Nabokumar was rooted to the spot spellbound. He could not decide whether to move before or behind. He had heard of Kapaliks and he knew the man to be a Kapalik.

When Nabokumar arrived, the Kapalik was so much engrossed either with worship or contemplation that he paid no attention to Nabokumar. After a long time he enquired in Sanskrit "who are you?"

"A Brahmin" replied Nabokumar.

"Wait" rejoined Kapalik and then slipped into his work which pre-occupied him. Nabokumar stood on his legs all the while.

Thus half the watch of the night passed away. At last, the Kapalik left his seat and said to Nabokumar in Sanskrit as before "Follow me."

It might be safely said that, at a time other than this, Nabokumar could hardly persuade himself to follow the Kapalik. But he was more dead than alive with hunger and thirst. So he said "I am under your Emimence' orders. But I am overcome with hunger and thirst. So kindly tell me where to get my food and drink."

"You are sent by Bhairobi" returned the Kapalik. "Follow me and you will be satisfied."

Nabokumar went behind the Kapalik. The two together walked a weary long distance. But none spoke on the way. At last they reached a hut overtopped with leaf-thatched cover. Kapaiik was the first to go inside and then invited Nabokumar within. He struck a light in a way mysterious to Nabokumar and enkindled a piece of wood. With the aid of light Nabokumar saw the cottage entirely built of Keya leaves. Within it were a few pieces of tiger-hides, a pitcher of water and some fruits and vegetables.

After lighting fire, the Kapalik said "You may help yourself to the fruits and vegetables. Drink the water from the pitcher in cup which you must make of tree-leaf and sleep, if you so mind, on the tiger-skin. Stay secure and have no fear from tiger. You shall meet me later on. Never leave this cottage until I see you again."

With these words, the Kapalik went away. Nabokumar having for his repast the few fruits and vegetables, and for his drink, the brackish water, was mightily pleased. He made his bed on the tiger-skin and after the day's troubles and worries fell into a sleep.

　　　　　　　　　　　　　　　BANKIM CHANDRA CHATTERJEE

V

On the sea-side

As soon as Nabokumar left his bed the next morning, he, as a matter of course, worried himself over going home; the more so, as the presence of the Kapalik boded evil. But, for the nonce, how was he to get out of this trackless forest? How would he strike out the right path that would take him home? The Kapalik was sure to know the way. Would he not, if asked, give him the direction? However, the Kapalik, so far he marked him, never showed in his manners anything wrong. Then why was he on earth to be afraid of him? On the other hand, the Kapalik warned him against leaving the cottage till the next meeting and that, if he now ran counter to his wishes, it might upset him. Nabokumar had heard that Kapaliks were capable of impossible feats. Then it was wrong of him to show any insubordination. After much anxious consideration, Nabokumar made up his mind, for the present, to remain within the cottage-bounds.

But by degrees, the day wore on. Still there was no sign of the Kapalik's return. Previous day's fast added to the privation all this time sharpened his hunger. The little store of fruits and vegetables had been eaten up overnight and now the hunger threatened to kill him in the event of his not leaving the hut-precincts in quest of fresh fruits and vegetables. Before the day faded away, hunger drove Nabokumar outdoor to seek out fruits, if he could find any.

Nabokumar wandered in and out between these neighbouring sand-dunes in search of fruit. He tried the fruits of one or two trees growing on the sands and found the fruit of only one tree had the delicious taste of almond. With these he satisfied his hunger.

The aforesaid sandhills were of small width and so Nabokumar surmounted these obstacles by a short detour. Then he entered a dense sandless forest. Those who, ever, for a short time have travelled an unknown wooded terrain know that the sense is confused almost immediately amidst the pathless forest-tract. The same happened to Nabokumar. After walking forward a little distance, he failed to pick out the way that led him there from the hermitage. The deep roll of rushing water met his ear and he learnt it to be the roar of the sea.

Soon after, which looked too sudden for him, he emerged from the forest-belt and saw the vision of the spreading sea before him. His heart thrilled with wild delights at the sight of the ever-stretching circle of deep blue water. He advanced and rested on the sandy beach. The foaming, blue, ever-spreading sea sprawled out before him. So far his eye could strike stretched away, both ways, the foam-line of the sea-surf cast up by the breaking splashing waves. The snowy foam-streaks were left deposited on the golden-yellow sands like a mass of milk-white flower garlands worked into fantastic shapes and figures. The waves breaking in foam at thousand places amidst the blue circle of water served meet decorations for the love-locks of the wood-tressed earth. If ever, there be the possibility of a fierce gale through whose violence the myriads of stars are displaced from their sockets and tossed up in the blue dome of the sky then it might conjure up the image of that breaking dashing sea. At this time, a portion of the saphire water shone like liquid gold in the mellow tints of the setting sun. At a far-off end a European merchant-man with her bulging white sails looked like a monster bird skipping over the surface of the water.

Nobokumar had no idea of the measure of time he spent in observing the beauty of the sea. Afterwards "grey-hooded" evening came and at once settled over the dark blue water. Then Nobokumar awoke to his sense and the idea was brought home to his mind of finding out the cottage. He drew a deep sigh and rose to his feet. No reason could be ascribed why he drew that sigh. But who could say there might not arise some happy thoughts in his mind of his joys in the days before? As he stood up he wheeled round moving his back upon the sea. No sooner did he jerk his head than behold! A beautiful silhouette—the delightful phantom of a radiant female form standing on the sandy fringe of the booming sea greeted his eyes in the waning light of the faded evening. The rich mass of her dishevelled hair fell in disordered profusion across her back and floating in clustering waves reached down below her waist-line. From amidst the dark silken tresses shone out an exquisite face that looked the beautiful painting framed in a fine setting. The face though partly hid under the thick heavy curls appeared like the envious gleams that lace the severing clouds. The glance of her big bright eyes was very quiet, very soft, very deep, though full of brilliance, shining like the streaks of moon-light playing across the glassy sea. The luxuriant tresses enveloped her neck and shoulders. Though the shoulders were fully concealed, the transparent colour of her arms, however, gleamed through the dense locks. The feminine figure was wholly denuded of any of the artificialities. The subtle charm pervading the beautiful figure can not be described in words. The happy graceful effects were heightened by the bold contrast of the rich complexion, which shone like the faint glow of a half-moon, to the raven-black of the dark hair, and, any attempt at conveying an adequate impression of the liquid graces, would fall far short of the reality if not actually perceived on the thundering sea-coast in the purple haze of grey twilight. Nabokumar stood root-bound at the sudden appearance of such a joyful vision in the midst of wilderness. His speech lost its articulation and he looked agape quivering with admiration. The maiden also stood standstill fixing the winkless steadfast gaze of her big wide eyes on Nabokumar's face. The difference between the two lay in the fact that Nabokumar had the startled look of a man lost in wonder while the damsel's stare showed no such evidence though it had the troubled air of anxiety in it.

Subsequently on this lonely sea-coast both kept on looking into each other's face. After a long time, the sweet tremulous voice of the damsel was heard softly enquiring "Traveller, have you lost your way?"—and at that musical voice all the magic wizardry was touched.

The flute of her treble voice swept a touch on a chord in Nobokumar's heart. At times, the wonderful gear of the heart-strings goes out of tune in such a way that with all our efforts no music can be struck out of them, though the defect can be remedied at the fine touch of a single word or the soft voice of a woman. Then everything becomes full of harmony and life an un-ending flow of music. The voice sent a drift into Nabokumar's ear in such sweet strains.

The melody rose in symphony and thrilled a music into Nabokumar's ear—"Traveller, have you lost your way?" The meaning failed him and he found no word of reply. The melody struck the air awhirl thrilling in wild ecstacy, floated through the evening sea-breeze that rustled in tree-leaves and died away in faint thin cadence until lost into the tumult of the sea.

The sea-girt earth was enchanting—the woman enrapturing—the voice thrilling—and the tune ran its whole gamut on heart's vibrating strings.

The maiden receiving no reply said "Follow." With these words, she moved forward with such light gait as could scarcely be visible. Like a fleecy cloud sent adrift by a gentle sigh of the spring, she advanced with slow, easy and unperceived steps with Nabokumar following behind mechanically like a doll working on spring-hinges. At one stage, the path wound round a copse and when Nobokumar was opposite to the thicket that intercepted his view, the fair guide gave him a slip and was lost sight of. Nabokumar hardly cleared the brushwood, when the cottage sprang to his eye.

VI

In the Kapalik's company

On entering the hut Nabokumar closed the door and sat down with the head on his hand. He did not lift his head for a long time.

"Is she a goddess?—or a woman in flesh and blood?—or a phantom of the Kapalik's creation?" were the thoughts uppermost in his mind as he sat immobile. He was at his wit's end.

Nabokumar was far too much occupied with his own thoughts to see any other object. A log of wood was burning in the cottage since before his return. Afterwardis, when far into night, it occurred to him that till then he had not performed his evening ceremonies, he struck up a truce with his cogitation in order to find out water. It was only then that the oddity forced itself upon his mind. Besides fire, there were rice and many other sundry things for the preparation of a meal. Nabokumar was not astonished at the sight of these as he believed them to be also the work of the Kapalik and at such a place as this it did not set him moping over it. Having finished the evening ceremonies, Nabokumar cooked the little rice in an earthen pot he found in the hut and had his repast.

As soon as he left his skin-bed the next morning, he struck for the sea-coast. The previous day's outing helped him in feeling his way before him with less difficulty. He performed his morning ceremonies there and stayed in a mood of expectancy. Whom did he expect? We are not sure how far the thought gained its ascendancy in Nabokumar's mind that the previously seen apparition would visit the place again but anyhow he could not leave the ground. However, no body came even when the day was far spent. Then Nabokumar fell into strollmg through the grounds. The search proved but fruitless.

He could not detect any trace of human footsteps. He came back again and sat himself down on the same spot. The sun went down and the shadows of evening were falling fast. Nabokumar, crestfallen, retraced his way to the habitation. On his return from the sea-side in the evening, he found the Kapalik silently squatted on the cottage floor. He first of all enquired about his health but the Kapalik made no rejoinder.

"Why was I denied your grace' visit all this time?" asked Nabokumar.

"I was engaged in my worship" replied the Kapalik.

Nabokumar made the proposal of return to his homelands. "Neither do I know the way nor have I the means" added he "but I counted on you as the line of action may be settled as soon as I see your worship again."

"Follow me" simply said the Kapalik. With this word, the hermit got up on his legs. Nabokumar, also, expecting that some feasible means of his return home might be devised, followed him.

The glow did not depart from the western sky, when Nabokumar was following the Kapalik who led the way. He, suddenly, felt the touch of some soft hand on his back and turning round stopped short at what he saw. It was the same wood-nymph with the glorious crown of rich silken tresses that clustered around her back—as speechless and immoveable as before.

From whence could the figure unexpectedly glide out behind him? Nabokumar saw the girl had a fingertip placed across her lips. He understood that the damsel warned him against the danger of speech. Was there any necessity for caution? He stood there agape wondering all the while. The Kapalik could not observe any of the enactments of this silent drama. So he moved onward. When they were out of the Kapalik's hearing, the maiden spoke something in an undertone. The words audible to Nabokumar were "Whither are you going? Desist—get back—flee."

Scarcely had the words issued from her lips when the fair speaker slipped away without waiting to hear the reply. Nabokumar stood there for sometime as one obsessed of a ghost. He yearned to follow in her wake. But he failed to strike the line of her escape. He thought within himself "Whose phantasy is this?—or is it the creation of my own mind?—what I heard is certainly frightful. But what the deuce do I care to be afraid of? Kapaliks can work miracles. Then shall I fly?—or why shall I fly?—when I lived the other day I must also live this day. The Kapalik is but a man, so I am too."

Nabokumar was meditating thus when he observed the Kapalik getting back as he could not see Nabakumar behind. "What makes you tarry?" asked the Kapalik. The Kapalik having re-iterated the question, Nabokumar without a word followed him. After walking a little distance Nabokumar's eyes rested on a cottage encircled with a mud-wall. The tenement struggled betweeh the debatable styles of a cottage and a small house. But with this we have no concern. Yonder over across the back-ground gleamed the rolling sand-downs. The Kapalik was leading Nabokumar to the sands along the edge of this hut. At this moment the previously seen damsel ran past Nabokumar with the quickness of an arrow. When alongside with him, she whispered into his ears "Escape yet. Don't you know Tantrick's rituals lose their merits if not supplemented by human flesh?"

Sweat started out on Nabokumar's forehead. As ill-luck would have it, the maiden's admonition entered the Kapalik's ear. "Kapalkundala" broke forth the Kapalik.

The voice fell upon Nabokumar's ear with the detonation of a thunder. But Kapalkundala did not answer.

The Kapalik conducted Nabokumar grasping him by his hand. The man-slayers' touch sent Nabokumar's blood coursing through his veins with a thousand-fold pulsation and his lost courage revived. "Leave off my hand" said Nabokumar. The Kapalik made no reply. "Where do you lead me to?" asked Nabokumar again. "To the place of worship" answered the Kapalik.

"Why" added Nabokumar.

"For immolation" joined the Kapalik. With a violent tug did Nabokumar pull out his hand. The force, with which Nabokumar jerked his hand, might have run an ordinary man down to the earth instead of allowing him to retain the hold on his hand. But not a part of the Kapalik's body bent and Nabokumar's hand was left in his grip as in a vice. The impact rebounded upon Nabokumar's system and sent a rattle through his bones. Nabokumar saw that strength would not avail but trick might serve the purpose. He allowed himself to be dragged along with the conclusion "Well, let me watch the flow of events."

When Nabokumar was led on to the central ground on the sands, he saw a log of wood crackling there as on the previous night. On all sides were arranged things adapted to the requirements of the Tantrick rites of worship including a human skull filled in with Ashab or wine. Only a human corpse was Wanting. He guessed his body would furnish the corpse.

A small stack of dry stout plants and creepers was piled up there from before-hand. The Kapalik began to bind Nabokumar tightly with these. Nabokumar exerted every ounce of his whole strength but his strength did not stand him in good stead. Nabokumar gained the belief that even at such an advanced age, the Kapalik could muster the strength of a mad elephant. Finding Nabokumar use violence, the Kapalik said "Fool, why do you pull your weight? The mass of your mortal flesh shall furnish the sacrifice for the Bhairobi worship. What a better luck than this can a man of your run expect?"

After fastly securing Nabokumar, the Kapalik laid him down on the sands and set himself to attend to the preparatory rites of worship. In the meantime Nabokumar tried to burst the bonds. But the dry creepers proved too strong and the knots too firm and he saw death before him. He resigned his soul to the sacred feet of his cherished god. The visions of his native land and his blessed home and the images of his long-lost parents passed before his mind in quick succession and a drop or two of scalding tears trickled down to the earth to be soaked into the parched sea-sands. Having finished the preliminary rites, the Kapalik left his seat to get his execution-axe. But he could not find the axe where it was kept. What a surprise! The Kapalik wondered a bit. He was cocksure that he brought the axe in the afternoon, put it at the right place and did not remove it anywhere else. Then what became of the axe? He conducted a hurried search here and there. But the axe could not be traced. Then facing the hut, he called out to Kapalkundala but despite repeated calls no answer came. Then the Kapalik's eyes inflamed and his eye-brows contracted. He hastened to the cottage-side. At the interval, Nabokumar made another attempt at bursting the binding creepers but that effort, too, shared its former fate.

At that time, hushed footfalls were heared pattering on the sands—not the heavy footsteps of the Kapalik. Nabokumar looked up the direction and saw the same enchantress Kapalkundala with the axe flourishing in her hand.

"Silence" enjoined Kapalkundala. "speak not—the axe is with me—I secreted it."

With these words Kapalkundala deftly set her hand to cutting open the creepers that made up Nabokumar's bondage. In a brace of seconds, she freed him and exhorted "Escape—follow me—I shall act the guide." Scarcely the words died on her lips when she vaulted forward and sped away like a bolt directing the way. Nabokumar, at a jump raced after her.

VII

In Quest

On the other hand, the Kapalik, after having had some hunting for the axe within the cottage-bounds, found neither the axe nor Kapalkundala. So he hastened back to the sands in a suspicious mood of mind. On his return he could not see Nabokumar there. At this, his astonishment grew intense. Soon after, his wandering eyes lighted on the broken bonds of creepers. Then the conviction was borne in upon him and he started out in search of Nabokumar. But it was impossible to make out in such a wilderness either the path or the direction the run-aways had taken. The visibility being low owing to darkness, he could not spot either of them. He moved about for sometime aiming at the sound of voice. But the voice was not audible everytime. So with the object of a close survey of the outlying grounds he mounted the crest of a sand-hill of a higher elevation. The Kapalik climbed the height from one side. He did not know that the base of the sand mound on the opposite side was worn-out and loose with rivulets of water running down in the rains. No sooner had the Kapalik got on the summit than the crown of the sand-hill in its tumble-down condition gave way under the heavy weight of his body and came down with a terrific crash. The falling debris dragged down the Kapalik along with it like a wild buffalo torn from its crest.

VIII

IN SHELTER

Under the wing of the inky darkness of the moonless night, both ran into cover of the wood at their top-most speed. The wood path was unknown to Nabokumar and he had no other choice left him than to follow the lead of that fair guide of sixteen summers. This, too, was writ on my brow by that unknown scribe thought he within himself. The reflection betrayed Nabokumar's ignorance that the Bengalee is always the slave and never the master of circumstances. If he even knew this, he would never have felt either sick or sorry for it. On they travelled, they gradually slackened their paces. The gloom enveloped everything under its deep fold. Only at places the chalky crests of sand-dunes seldom loomed sentinel-like under the star-lit night. At odd intervals, in the tiny glow of the fire-flies, the tall trees of the forest stood out in their ghostly outlines against the dark blue sky.

Nabokumar in company of Kapalkundala arrived at a lonely recess in the wood. The turret of a temple was descried in the foreground through the forest gloom. Near the temple was, also, visible a house with a brick wall around it. Advancing, Kapalkundala knocked at the door in the wall and after short sharp raps came out a man's voice from inside "I presume you are Kapalkundala." "Open the door please" chimed in, Kapalkundala.

The speaker came down and unfastened the door. The man who threw open the door looked either the care-taker or the owner of the edifice raised to the Goddess inside, and appeared to have been on the wrong side of fifty. Kapalkundla with both hands drew the thin-haired head of the man near her lips and explained in a whispering word or two the plight of the stranger. The proprietor or the Adhicary of the shrine placing the head on his hand revolved the question in his mind for a long time.

"It is a serious affair" observed the man at length. "The saintly man can work miracles. However, through the grace of the Mother Goddess no misfortunes can befall you. Where is the man?"

"Come in" trilled out Kapalkundala to Nabokumar. Thus invited, Nabokumar who kept himself well under cover slipped into the house.

"Hide your head for the night here" said the Adhicary to him. "Before the day breaks tomorrow I shall put you on the Midnapore highway."

The Adhicary in course of conversation gathered that Nabokumar till then had not had a morsel of food. So he bustled himself arranging for Nabokumar's repast. But Nabokumar showed his disinclination to have had any food at all and simply prayed for the resting place. The Adhicary made Nabokumar's bed in his own kitchen-room. After Nabokumar had laid himself down to rest, Kapalkundala was making herself ready to get back to the sea-shore.

The Adhicary eyeing her affectionately said "Don't go. Rest a while. I have a request."

"What you mean?"

"Since these eyes saw you, I have begun to call you mother and I can swear by the feet of the Goddess that I love you more than my own mother. Won't you keep my request?"

"Certainly, I will."

"My only request is that you must not get back there any more."

"Why?"

"If you go, you are undone."

"That I know too."

"Then what makes you question again."

"Where am I to go, if not there?"

"Go forth into otherland in company of this stranger."

Kapalkundala remained silent.

"What gives you furiously to think over it, mother?" asked the Adhicary.

"When your disciple came, you urged the immorality of my accompanying, as a young maid, another young man. But why do you tell me to do so again?"

"Then your life was not in jeopardy. Besides, the opportunity, which was lacking men, might prove golden now. Come, let us have the sanction of our Mother.

Saying this, the Adhicary holding a lighted lamp in his hand issued forth and went over to the temple porch and opened the door. Kapalkundala, also, went behind him. Inside the temple was established the frightful Goddess Kali of the height and measure of a human figure. Both bent low before her in deep reverence. The Adhicary, after going through the holy preliminaries and reciting incantations in invocation of the deity, took a trident leaf from the flower stand and placing it at the feet of the Goddess looked intently on it. Shortly after, the Adhicary remarked to Kapalkundala "Look, mother, the Goddess has accepted the offering as the trident leaf has not dropped down. The idea with which the offering has been made is sure to materialise favourably. Go forth with this foreigner with a light heart. But I know the manners and conduct of the worldly people. If you literally prove a dead weight round his neck, then a blush might rise to the cheeck of this stranger to have a young girl by him in society. Besides, the world might treat you contemptuously. You say this man is a Brahmin and I see, too, he has a sacred thread around his neck. If this man takes you home after marriage then it is happy and good. Otherwrise I can never advise you to bear him company."

Kapalkundala slowly drawled out the word "M-a-r-r-i-a-g-e."

"I heard the word 'Marriage' from your lips" went on she, "but have never understood the honest meaning of the expression. What's to be done?"

The Adhicary gave a silent and slight laugh and said "To woman wedlock is but a stepping stone to the soul's flight to holihead and for this she is called the better-half of man. Even, the Mother of the Universe is Shiva's married wife."

The temple-keeper thought he explained everything and Kapalkundala thought he understood everything.

"Let it be as you say" added Kapalkundala. "But my heart is loth to let him severely alone as he brought me up by hand for so long a time."

"You don't know why he reared you."

After this, the Adhicary or temple-keeper made a feeble attempt at making a half-hearted exposition to Kapalkundala as to the relation of woman to the Tantrick rites of worship. Though Kapalkundala could not take in all this, still a chill gripped her heart.

"Let me be led to the marriage altar then" stammered out she.

Afterwards, both went out of the temple. The temple-keeper, making Kapalkundala wait in a room, approached Nabokumar's bed and sat at the head of the bed-stead.

"Sir" enquired he "are you asleep?"

Nabokumar was not in a mood to fall into a sleep. He lay brooding over his own condition.

"No, Sir" answered he.

"Sir, I have turned in here" resumed the Adhicary "to gather your particulars. May I ask if you are a Brahmin?"

"Oh! yes, I am."

"Of what sect?"

"Of Rahri sect."

"I, too, belong to the Rahri order of Brahmins. So, please, never take me for a Brahmin that came of the Uriya stock. By family pedigree, I am a first-rate Kulin though, for the present, I have taken refuge under the foot-stool of the Mother Goddess. Your name please."

"Nabokumar Sharma."

"Native village?"

"Saptagram."

"Of what branch of Kulins?"

"Bandoghati."

"How many times did you marry?"

"For the first time."

Nabokumar did not lay bare his whole heart. In fact, he had no wife at all. He married Padmabati, the daughter, of Ram Govinda Ghosal. After marriage Padmabati stayed at her father's place for a short time and at times visited her father-in-law's house. Her father had been on a holy pilgrimage to Puri with the whole family when she was barely thirteen. At this time, the Pathans who were expelled from Bengal by Akbar found an asylum in Orissa. Akbar had quite a tough job to quell them. The Moghuls and Pathans had been on their war-path when Ram Govinda Ghosal was getting back from Orissa. On the way he fell into the hands of the Pathans, who, at that time, were in the habit of trampling down the codes of war etiquette and so used violence to innocent passers to squeeze out money. Ram Govinda was of choleric temper so he abused the Pathans. The up-shot was that he with the whole family was thrown into prison. At last he and the family changed faith and were released on their apostasy. Though Ram Govinda and the family returned home unhurt, they were treated as outcasts by the relation and society. Nabokumar's father was living and he discarded his daughter-in-law as well as her father who had cast away the faith. Nabokumar did not any more set his eyes on his wife. Renounced by the relation and society, Ram Govinda could not hold his head high in his native village for long. What with these grounds and what with his high ambition to secure some fat billet through royal favour did Ram Govinda move to Rajmahal with his family and settled there. Having turned renegades, he and the family adopted Mussulmun names. Since they repaired to Rajmahal, Nabokumar had no means of knowing the whereabouts of either the wife or the father and so far he received no news about them. Nabokumar was reluctant any more to take to second wife. For this, we are entitled to say that Nabokumar had no wife at all. Adhicary was not aware of all this. He concluded that there might be no harm for a Kulin's son to be a polygamist.

"I came to tell you one thing," he spoke aloud. "This girl who saved your life has sacrificed her own life for other's good. The saintly man under whose protection she lives is a horrid being. If she goes back she needs must share the same fate as you were almost doing. May I ask whether you can suggest any way out of this?"

Nabokumar sat up on the bed-stead.

"I, too, feared that," said he. "You know everything so you can suggest the means. If my self-immolation can repay any thing, I am ready to sacrifice myself. I have so made up my mind as to return to the man-slayer and surrender myself to him. In that case her life may be spared."

The Adhicary laughed silently.

"You are insane," said he. "What would this result in? The flame of your life would be put out though it would not extinguish the wrath of the personage. It admits but of one solution."

"What is it?"

"It means her flight with you. But that, too, is a risky adventure. If you tarry in my place any longer, you are sure to be apprehended in a day or two. That saintly man frequents this holy shrine. So it portends misfortunes to Kapalkundala."

"What risk is there" returned Nabokumar quick with eagerness "in her escape with me?"

"You don't know this girl's parents and lineage—whose wife she is and of what character? Would you take her as your companion? Granting you take her as your companion in life, would you shelter her under your paternal roof? Besides, if you refuse her any asylum where would this orphan go?"

Nabokumar reflected for sometime and joined "I shall not let the grass grow under my feet to be of any service to my saviour. She shall find a place in the inner ring of my family."

"Well and good. But when the people would come and ask whose wife she is what answer would you give?"

Nabokumar mused again and added "You must tell me that and I will say to each and every one accordingly."

"Good. But how is it possible for a young man and a young maid to go together alone on a fortnight's journey? what will men say to all this? How would you explain it to your friends and relatives? Besides, when I have called this girl my mother, does it behove me to pack her off to a far-off country in company of stranger?"

The prince of match-makers was not ill-adept in match-making.

"Be pleased then to come with us" urged Nabokumar.

"Indeed! Then who would offer Pujah to the Goddess Bhowani?"

Nabokumar was at a quandary and replied "Can't you point then to any solution to this riddle?"

"There may be one and only one solution that waits upon your generosity."

"What might it be? In what do I not acquiesce in? Please tell me the way out."

"Listen. She is the daughter of a Brahmin father. In her infancy, she was carried away by the wicked pirates but was abandoned on the sea-coast due to ship-wreck. You will have the details from her later on. Chance had given her over to the Kapalik who nursed and tended her so that his ritualism might attain its fruition. He could, by this time, have encompassed his own end but affection forged a fetter that held him with a hand of iron. Marry her and take her home so that none will have their say. I shall conduct the marriage according to scriptural rites."

Nabokumar rose on his legs and paced up and down with quick steps silently.

"Take your bed now" resumed the Adhicary after a brief interval. "I shall wake you up early tomorrow morning. If you like, you may go alone. I shall place you on the Midnapore high-way."

With these words, the Adhicary took leave. While retiring, he thought within "Is it that I have forgotten the ways of marriage negotiations in Western Bangal?"

IX

In the holy shrine

The Adhicary hastened back to Nabokumar at day-break and found that he did never take his bed for the night.

"What is advisable now?" asked he.

"From this day forward" said Nabokumar "she shall be made and remain my lawful wife. If the act needs the renunciation of the world I am ready to do so for her sake. Who will give her hand away in marriage?"

The face of the man of the first-rate match-making abilities beamed up with joy.

"After so long, O Mother of the Creation, perhaps, my hapless daughter's star has risen" thought the Adhicary within himself.

"I shall bestow her upon you in the marriage ceremony" said he aloud. Then the Adhicary re-entered his bed-room. An old piece of cloth wrapped some ancient worm-eaten palm-leaves. Within it was preserved an astrological record of the stellar movements and positions. He drew up a chart, made minute calculations and then came out and said "Though the day is not auspicious enough for nuptials, yet there can be no harm in disposing of her hand in marriage. I shall hand her to you in the twilight moments and you shall have only to keep fasting the whole day. Do the sacred family rites at home. I have a place where I can hide you for a day only. If he happens to look in here in the course of day-light hours, he shall have no scent of you. After the marriage is over, you can, with your wife, leave the place next morning."

Nabokumar agreed to the proposal. Shastric observances were followed as far as practicable in the circumstances. On the border line between light and darkness did Nabokumar lead to the marriage altar the ascetic girl, nursed by the Kapalik. So far no news reached them of the Kapalik. The following morning, the trio prepared for the journey. It had been settled that the Adhicary would accompany them as far as the Midnapore high-road. Against departure, Kapalkundala went to make her last obeisance to the Goddess Kali. After she had devotedly bowed down her head, she took a trident leaf, whole and unbroken, from the flower basket and placing it at the feet of the idol, intently gazed down at it. The leaf dropped down. Kapalkundala was intensely religious. She was horror-struck to see the trident leaf slip away from the feet of the holy figure and so informed the Adhicary who was aggrieved to hear of it.

"Now there is no help for it," said he. "You have been united in holy bonds so you must follow your husband to the funeral pyre if it is so needed. Go forth silently."

All of them moved noiselessly forward. The morning waxed hot when they arrived at the Midnapore high-road. Here the Adhicary bade farewell to the party whereupon Kapalkundala burst into a rain of tears. The only friend, she had in this wide world over, was taking his final leave. The Adhicary also felt a mist rising over his eyes. He brushed the tears from Kapalkundala's eyes and whispered into her ears "Mother, you know, through the grace of the Mother of the Universe, your son stands in no need of wealth. Both the high and low of the Hijli country-side bow their knees to the Goddess and send in their offerings. Give your husband what I have tied to your cloth-end and tell him to hire a palanquin for you and ever and always remember your son."

The Adhicary retired from the scene with streaming eyes. Kapalkundala, as well, went her way with her sight bedimmed with tears.

PART II

I

On the highway

On his arrival at Midnapore, Nabokumar engaged a maid-servant, an escort and palanquin bearers for Kapalkundala through Adhicary's money and sent her away on the road before him in the palanquin. He, himself, tramped along on account of the scantiness of his purse. He felt much fatigued on account of the worries of the day before, and so the palanquin bearers out-distanced him a long way after mid-day meal. Gradually the evening drew near. The wintry sky was littered over with light-grey clouds that threatened rain. By degrees, the evening wore away into night that was settling down upon the earth with the mantle of darkness closing in upon everything. A thin rain began to fall in drib drabs. Nabokumar bustled forward to join Kapalkundala. He had the firm conviction that he would meet with her at the first road-side inn but so far no inn fell upon his eyes. The night was deepening. Nabokumar threw in an extra energy into his gait. Suddenly his feet came upon something hard and uneven. The thing crashed into splinters under the weight of his body and a dry crackle leapt to his ears. He stopped short and then moved onward again. Again the same crack met his ears. He picked up the trampled-down things and found them appearing like pieces of broken bed-stead. Even when the sky is cloudy it never gets dark enough for material things not to be seen lying in front in the open. A large object lay on the ground in front of him and he felt it to be the broken part of palanquin boards. Scarcely had he perceived this than a suspicion crossed his mind that Kapalkundala might be in danger. He hastened towards the direction of the travelling palanquin when his feet touched some objects of a different category. It was like the soft touch of a human body. He sat down and moved his hand across the surface of the object. The impression gained confirmed his suspicion. The touch felt cold and icy and brought along with it the perception of some liquid flow. He felt for the pulse but could not find any as life had been extinct. He surveyed the thing in the darkness with increased attention and thought he heard some breathing sound. If the breath is left then why the pulse does not beat? Is it a sickman? He put his hand near the nose but perceived no respiration. Then where did the sound come from? Might be some living humanity happens to be here. Thinking thus he enquired at the top of his voice. "Is there any living man here?"

Softly a murmuring answer came "yes."

"Who are you?" asked Nabokumar.

"Who are you?" echoed back the reply.

The voice seemed to be the voice of a woman. Quick with eagerness Nabokumar querried "Are you Kapalkundala?"

"I don't know who is Kapalkundala," replied the woman. "I am a traveller and have been robbed of my Kundalas (ear-pendants), for the present, by the high way robbers."

Nabokumar was somewhat flattered with the joke in the form of a pun and asked "What is the matter with you?"

"The robbers smashed my palanquin" said the answering voice "and killed a bearer as the rest stampeded. The rascals carried away all the ornaments I had on my person and tied me to the palanquin."

Nabokumar saw through the haze of darkness that actually a woman remained there bound up with the palanquin. He undid the fastenings with quick fingers and interrogated "Can you rise?"

"One stroke fell upon me," said the woman. "So I feel a burning pain in my leg. But, I think, with a little help I can rise on my legs."

Nabokumar stretched a helping hand. The woman got up with the assistance.

"Can you walk?" enquired he.

"Have you seen any other traveller coming behind you!" brusquely asked the woman without answering the question?

"No" replied Nabokumar.

"How far is the inn?" questioned the woman again.

"I am not sure how far it is." said he "But more possible than not it is close by."

"What good is there in sitting on alone on such a wild heath in darkness?" added the woman. "It is better, certainly, to follow you into the inn. I think I can walk over the distance if I get any support."

"It is foolish to fight shy in the hour of danger" joined he. "Please lean on my shoulder and move along."

The woman did not play the fool. She walked forward with Nabokumar's assistance. As a matter of fact, the inn stood at an easy distance. In those days, the robbers feared not to ply their dirty trade at a close radius from the inn. Before it was long, Nabokumar arrived at the estaminet followed by the woman. He found Kapalkundala placed at the same inn where her people appointed a room for her. He engaged the adjoining room for his companion and lodged her in it. At his bidding, the land-lady brought in a lamp. When the flood of light fell upon the person of his fair companion, he was startled to find her an uncommon beauty. Like the full-coursed river overflowing its bank in the rains, the profuse full-blown graces of her exquisitely modelled youthful figure threw in an indescribable charm and created an atmosphere of loveliness around her.

II

At the inn

If this woman happened to have been reproachlessly beautiful then I might venture the remark "Gentleman reader, she is as much beautiful as your sweetheart, and, fair reader, she is just your shadow reflected in your looking glass." This would have been pen-pourtraying to its finish. Unfortunately she was not a faultless beauty. So I have to resist the temptation. The reason in saying that she was not a perfect beauty is, first, she was a trifle taller than the average medium figure,—secondly, her upper and lower lips slightly curled up inwards, and, thirdly, she had not a complexion of cream-and-rose. Though comparatively of a taller height, her body was full of a buxom bosom and her limbs showed perfect fulness and rotundity. As in the rains the cringing creeper sways majestically with its green gorgeous foliage, so her form displayed all the infinite graces on account of the lusty fulness of life. As a matter of course, her figure, though, to some degree, a shade taller in size, looked all the more resplendent because of its full-blooded roundness. Amongst the class of beauties of the really milk-and-rose style, some wears the hue of the liquid silver of the full moon and some the colour of the russet-tinted dawn. She had none of the complexions of the above two categories, so we can never say she had actually any brilliancy of skin though in magic effects her charms played no less a potency. She was a little darker. But that never suggests the blackness, of which Shyama's mother or Shyama, the good-looking, is the type. The transparency of her skin had as much sparkle as the glow of the dissolved gold. If the white splendour of the full-moon or the first flush of the saffron-coloured dawn be taken the criteria of the skin of the dainty eves, then the refreshing yellow-and-green of the new shafts of mango blossoms shooting up in the divinest of seasons may be made the comparing standard of this damsel's complexion. If amongst readers there might be many who are chivalrous enough to press the claims of the olive-complexioned beauties to the fore-front, and, also, as chance would have it, there might be anyone whose smitten soul has been left to the care of a dark-skinned witch, then the latter in any case can never be called colour-blind. If any body is offended at this, let him paint before his mind's eye the dark silky locks kissing the bright forehead like the deep rows of black bees lining the new-blown mango blossoms—let him imagine the pair of arched eye-brows under a shapely fore-head, as beautiful as a three-quarter silvery moon, overblown by ringlets—let him idealise the smooth velvety cheeks of the rich mellowed hues of golden mangos—let him pourtray a couple of small thin red lips like two streaks of scarlet, and, it is then, that he might have the impression of this fair stranger as the queen of beauty. Her eyes, though not wide, were full of brilliance and fringed with bowed lashes. The glance was steady but keen and searching. When the eyes are fixed upon you, you, at once, feel that this woman is probing the bottom of your heart. By degrees, the glaring intensity is apt to melt and the looks soften and become mellifluously affectionate. Sometimes, again, they bespeak certain languor and lassitude, born of voluptuous abandonment, appearing the soft dreamy bed of the blind baby-god with bow and arrows. At times, the eye-balls expand and dilate hot with desires full of amorous coyness. Again, they shoot up, at intervals, some sinister side-long glances resembling vivid flashes amidst dark clouds.

The face was lit up with two fine expressions—first, the forcefulness of an all-mastering intelligence,—secondly, an over-weening conceit. So, when she chanced to stand up imperiously and bend her swan-neck, she looked the right royal type of the feminist. She passed her seven-and-twenty summers—she the torrential river of the rich, ripe, golden autumn that has but set in. Her charms flowed and sparkled full to the brim, ready to break over the contents. The ripening fulness of those graces was more soul-enrapturing than the colour, the eye and all else besides. In her youthful sleekness, the whole frame coloured and quivered with a virility like the autumnal river sheening and shimmering under the gentlest sigh of a wind and the graceful rippling spread out the charms in all their shifting colours and contours.

Nabokumar with eager eyes was gazing upon this glorious form with all the changing shades of beauties. The fair creature caught sight of Nabakumar's hard stare and watchful speculating eyes. "What do you look into intently?" asked she "My beauty?"

Nabokumar was gentle-born. He felt awkward and hung down his head in shame.

Seeing him silent, she archly remarked "Have you not ever seen a woman?—Or you think me an extraordinary beauty?"

Naturally, this might have amounted to a reproach. But the radiant smile that accompanied the words, took off the biting sting. So it savoured more of a jest than anything else. Nabokumar saw her tongue had sharp edges. hen why should he not reply her sharp remark ?

"I have seen many a woman" answered he "but never such a beautiful one."

The woman boastfully asked "Not a single one?"

The soft sweet charms of Kapalkundala floated before Nabokumar's mind, and, he, too, proudly returned "Not a single one! No—I can never say that."

"So far so good" rejoined the woman. "Is she your wife?"

"Why? What above all things sends you on the thought of a wife?"

"The Bengalee always regards his wife as an unsurpassed beauty."

"I am a true-born Bengalee. But you, too, speak the Bengali dialect. To what country else do you belong then?"

The damsel glanced at her own style of dress and said "As ill-luck would have it, this hapless self is not a Bengalee woman but an up-country Mussalmani."

Nabokumar eyed her up and down and saw the dress exactly suited the up-country fashion, though she was speaking the Bengali as much chastely as a born Bengalee.

After a short spell the young woman resumed "Sir, you have gathered all the information about me by parry of words. Now be pleased to let me know your own particulars. May I enquire the place where that incomparable beauty rules the house-hold?"

"Saptagrain is my native land" replied Nabokumar.

The foreigner added no answer. Suddenly she bent her head and plied her fingers brightening up the lamp-light.

Shortly after, without raising her head, she softly broke in "The servant's name is Moti. May I have the pleasure of knowing your name?"

"Nabokumar Sharma" said Nabokumar.

The light was blown out by a deep sigh and a hush fell in the room.

III

Meeting with the beautiful woman

Nabokumar ordered the inn-keeper for another light. He had heard a deep sigh before another light was brought in. A few minutes later, a Mussulman in servant's livery made his appearance. At his sight, the foreigner burst out "Eh! What made you delay so much? Where are others gone?"

"The palanquin bearers were all drunk" meekly joined the servant "and as I had to collect them together, I lagged behind. Afterwards, the broken palanquin and your disappearance frightened us out of our wits. Some men are left on the spot and others conducting the search in different directions. I turned in in this quarter on a scent."

"Conduct them before me" rang out the silver voice of Moti.

The servant made a deep bow and retired. The fair stranger remained seated for sometime, resting the head on her hand. Nabokumar asked leave to withdraw and then Moti shook herself as if coming out of a reverie. Without relinquishing her previous pose, she asked "Where are you going to put up for the night?"

"The room next to this."

"I saw a palanquin there. Have you any companion with you?"

"My wife is with me."

It gave another opportunity of showing Moti's vein of humour.

"Is she the non-pareil beauty" asked Moti.

"When you see, you will guess it" replied Nabokumar.

"May these eyes see her?"

(In thoughtful air) "What harm is there?"

"Then be pleased to show me this favour. My curiosity to see this peerless beauty has been piqued to the extreme. I shall carry the tale to Agra—but it is not befitting the time—good-bye for the present. I shall send you information afterwards."

Nabokumar left the place. Soon after, a troop of retainers with a retinue of servants and servant-maids, with kits, and bags and baggages appeared on the scene. A palanquin, too, accompanied them with a chamber-maid inside it.

Later on, the news reached Nabokumar "The mistress has remembered you." Nabokumar reappeared before Moti. He saw a new departure this time. Moti changed and made a fresh toilet. She put on her embroidered garments splashed with gold and pearls and garnished her unadorned figure with ornaments. The enamel-works of diamonds, rubies and other precious stones on the gold ornaments worn on every available inch of space on the body—the side-locks, the braided knot, the brow, the temple, the ears, the neck, the bosom the arms and the shoulders—glinted in ten thousand glittering points and dazzled the eyes of Nabokumar. Like the countless stars bespangling the sky, the innumerable gems setting off the exquisite charms and contours of the splendid figure heightened the effects which blended in a harmonising whole were thrown off into boldest relief.

"Sir, let me be conducted and introduced to your wife" said Moti to Nabokumar.

"There is no use wearing jewelleries like that" joined Nabokumar. "Of ornaments my wife has none at all."

"But what does it matter if I deck my person to display my jewellery? Women possessing jewelleries can not help making a show of them. Let us go now."

Nabokumar showed her the way. The woman who had ridden the palanquin also accompanied them. Her name was Peshman. Kapalkundala was seated alone on the wet ground of the shop-room. The faint glimmer of a lamp-light made the darkness visible only. Her rich mass of untied hair fell in a heap and darkened her back. At the first sight, the feeble ray of a faint smile glistened in the eyes and flickered on the lips of Moti. To get a closer view, did Moti hold aloft the light and bring it near Kapalkundala's face and then the flicker of the smile fled away. Moti's expressions hardened up in a rigid setting and she gazed on throbbing with admiration, holding her bated breath in aesthetic enjoyment. None spoke—Moti charmed and spell-bound and Kapalkundala touched with surprise. Afterwards Moti began to pull off the ornaments from her own person. She denuded her body of all the jewelleries and proceeded to place these one by one on Kapalkundala's person. Kapalkundala did not speak a word all this time.

"What you mean by all this?" exclaimed Nabokumar in wonder. But Moti made no rejoinder.

After finishing the work on hand, Moti said "You told me a perfect truth. Such a flower never blooms in a king's garden. The regret is I can not show this blooming beauty in the capital. These jewelleries are befitting such a frame-work. So I set these on her. You, too, I hope, will be-deck her person, at times, with these and remember this sharp-tongued stranger."

Nabokumar was amazed and said "How is it? These jewelleries are worth a king's ransom. How can I accept these?"

"Through Providence' kindness, I have more of these and I shall never have the occasion to miss them. If I feel any happiness in embellishing her what on earth might be the reason of your objecting?"

With this, Moti left the place in company of her dressing maid. When they had reached some removed ground Peshman asked Moti "Dear Lady, who is he?"

"My dearest" answered the Mussalmani mistress.

IV

IN THE PALANQUIN

N ow let us have the story of the ornaments. Moti made a present of an ivory box inlaid with silver for the preservation of ornaments. The robbers carried off only a small booty—they laid their violent hands on the articles she had near her person but nothing more than these. Nabokumar left one or two ornaments on Kapalkundala's body and put away the rest in the jewel-box. Moti left for Burdwan the next morning and Nabokumar with Kapalkundala went forth towards Saptagram. Placing Kapalkundala in the palanquin, Nabokumar put the jewel—box with her. The bearers, as a matter of course, trotted off at a fast pace and left Nabokumar a long way behind. Kapalkundala opened the palanquin doors and looked about enjoying the landscape. A beggar espied her and followed the palanquin droning piteously for alms.

"I have nothing with me" said Kapalkundala "So what can I give you?"

The beggar pointed to one or two ornaments Kapalkundala had on and said "How strange, mother! Pearls and diamonds gleam and glitter on your person and you have nothing to give away?"

"Are you satisfied if you get these?" asked Kapalkundala.

The beggar was stupefied. He pitched his aspiration a point higher and in a trice added "Of course I do."

Without a second thought, Kapalkundala gave away the jewel-box with all the jewelleries into the beggar's hands. She even tore off a few ornaments she had on her and made a gift of these. The beggar stared for a moment, with those droll expressions peculiar to the class. The servants and servant-maids did not have a scent of all this. The beggar's bewildered expression was, however, of a moment's duration. Immediately he gave his furtive glances all the country round and at a bound ran off with the ornaments.

"What made the beggar dash away for his dear life?" thought Kapalkundala.

V

In his native land

Nabokumar returned home with Kapalkundala. He had no father though he had his widowed mother and two sisters. The first sister was also a widow and we shall have no occasion to introduce our gentle reader to her. The second one was Shyamasundari. She had her husband alive though she looked a widow to all intents and purposes as she had been married to a high-class Kulin. She alone will make her appearance in our midst once or twice. We are not sure how far Nabokumar's relations would have been satisfied if he chanced to marry an ascetic girl and carried her home in a changed set of circumstances. After all, Nabokumar encountered no difficulty in this respect as every body despaired of his return.

On return home, his erstwhile companions bruited it far and wide that Nabokumar was killed by a tiger. The gentle reader may think that these people who bore the hall-mark of veracity invented the story according to their own beliefs and opinions. If this be his honest opinion, then he does a grave injustice to the fantastic inventiveness of these wise acres. Of the returned pilgrims, many made solemn affirmations that they saw with their own eyes Nabokumar run into the jaw of the tiger. At times, long-winded frothy debates were held as to the size of the tiger. Some asseverated that the tiger measured twelve feet but others negatived the idea and solemnly affirmed that the beast measured close upon one-and-twenty feet. Our previous acquaintance, the old pilgrim, said "It seems I have had a clean shave. The tiger took its first spring towards me but I showed him a clean pair of heels. Anyhow, Nabokumar was not such a daring spirit so he could not make off."

When all these versions reached the ears of Nabokumar's mother and relations they set up such a howl as raged with unabated fury for days end-on. Nabokumar's mother was stricken down with grief at the news of the bereavement of her only son. Just at this psychological moment the son made his way back home with his newly married wife. Now there was none in the whole countryside who dared raise issues on the topics of his bride's caste and origin! Every body was overjoyed to see him come back. Nabokumar's mother gave the bride a hearty reception and after the performance of the requisite after-marriage ceremonies carried her home shoulder-high. His joy passed all bounds on seeing Kapalkundala warmly received within his home circle. Even when he won Kapalkundala's hand he betrayed not the least sign of joy or affection fearing a cold shoulder might be given the party at home which might serve the damper. Still the thoughts of Kapalkundala filled his whole mental horizon. This was the only consideration weighing with Nabokumar that explained his shyness to close in with the offer of the proferred hand of Kapalkundala—that precluded his utterance of a single endearing term for a single time to Kapalkundala even when he got back home after marriage and, lastly, that prevented the smallest wave to ruffle the calm surface of his rising sea of love and affection. But the fear that haunted him all this time was now gone for ever. As a rushing stream gathering its volume before an obstacle in its path crashes down with redoubled fury when that impediment is dislodged so the growing enthusiastic love of Nabokumar surged and broke over all restraints. These pregnant feelings of affection though not often expressed in words could be read in Nabokumar's glistening ardent gaze upon Kapalkundala every time she chanced to cross his line of vision—in his constant visits to Kapalkundala on the pretext of urgency on the most trivial grounds—in his hovering around Kapalkundala without any occasion for it—in his attempts at driving at the topic of Kapalkundala in the midst of conversation without any necessity for it— in his ceaseless efforts to encompass Kapalkundala with all the comforts and well-being of home-life—and, in fine, in his halting gait of walk due to the distraction of his mind. Even his tone of life underwent some change. An air of seriousness settled in place of buoyant sportiveness— vivacity supplanted languor and Nabokumar's face brightened up at all times with joy. The heart being the mainspring of love, it blossomed into greater and nobler things. His love grew for all others—his tolerance extended to the undesirables—his heart overflowed with the milk of human kindness towards all mankind—the earth appeared the creation for piety and goodness and everything looked joyful and radiant. Such is love. It gives its colouring to everything. It sweetens harshness—turns iniquity into virtue—gives a halo to unholiness and ushers light into darkness. But what about Kapalkundala? In what mood is she now? Well, reader, let us go and have a look at her.

VI

In domestic seclusion

Every body is aware that Saptagram was a city of considerable importance in her past days. Once she formed the trysting ground of maritime traders of every clime from Java to Rome. But her old splendours were much on the wane between the Bengali 10th and 11th centuries. Its main reason was that the river that washed the edge of the city was shrunk up in its channel so that sailing crafts of larger draughts could not push up well within her harbour. So she lost much of her commercial importance. A city of commercial greatness loses everything with the loss of her commercial glory. Such was the ease with Saptagram.

Hooghly, in the 11th century, was leaping into existence and fame as her rival with all her nascent glories. The Portuguese established their business houses there which drew the wealth and opulence of Saptagram. But till then Saptagram was not shorn of all the vestiges of her fallen greatness. She still formed the headquarters of Fouzdars and other important Government officials though a large area of the city lost much of her attractiveness and, being uninhabited, gradually wore the aspect of a village.

Nabokumar's house was situated in an out-of-the-way nook on the periphery of Saptagram. The streets in her much ruined state were sequestered and overgrown with shrubs and trailers. In the background of Nabokumar's dwelling place lay a thick forest. A small stream ran across a mile's distance in the fore-ground that meandering its course around a small field entered the wood. The house was brick-built though on an all-round consideration it did not rise much above the common-place. Although double-storied, it was not enormously high and so could not have any pretension to a mansion. Its specimen height can, now-a-days, be seen in the basement in many instances.

Two young women stood on the house-top and were viewing the country round below. The house was framed in a beautiful setting. It was evening and the landscape was really beautiful and fascinating. Close by, lay the dense woodland with the innumerable feathered choristers singing their piping chorus inside with the rivulet flowing at a distance, looking a thin silver ribbon. Yonder across the grounds unrolled the panoroma of landscape and town where gleamed ten thousand edifices of the vast city the windows and casements of which were thronged with citizens eager to have an airing in the soft breeze of the fresh spring. Far away on the otherside, were the shadows of the evening thickening over the broad water of the Bhagirathi crowded with sailing smacks.

Of the young women on the terrace, the complexion of one had the gleam of the moon-shine. Her figure was half-concealed amidst her loose dark tresses. The other dark-skinned and of clear-cut features was neither just in nor well out of her gushing sixteen. She was thin and small. Her small ringlets were blown-over the upper half of her tiny face like the petals of a full-blown lotus encircling the cup in the centre. Her eyes were large and of a mild white as of the fish. Her tiny fingers were enmeshed in her companion's flowing mass of curling hair. Our presumption is at par that the reader has recognised the girl with the tint of the silver moon-beam to be our Kapalkundala. We may let him understand, besides, that the dark-complexioned one is her sister-in-law, Shyamasunari.

Shyamasundari was addressing her brother's wife at times as 'Bow' (brother's wife), sometimes endearingly as sister and at other times as Mrino. The name Kapalkundala was a bit horrible so women-folk called her Mrinmoyee. We, too, shall hence forward call her by this name though not too often. Shyamasundari was reciting verses from a nursery poem:

> *They say the lotus-queen that veils her*
> *face when falls the night*
> *Makes buds to ope and bees to flee as her*
> *dear lord's in sight.*
> *With leaves spread-out to the tree the*
> *woodland creeper flies,*
> *So the river stream when comes the*
> *flood to the ocean hies.*
> *O, what a shame the bashless lily blooms*
> *when the moon doth shine,*
> *And the newly wedded bride, her wedlock*
> *o'er, does for her husband pine.*

Shyamasundari. "Would you lead an ascetic's single life all your days?" "Why? what asceticism do I practise?" replied Mrinmoyee.

Shyamasundari with both hands lifting Mrinmoyee's rich curling locks exclaimed "Would you never gather this heap of hair in a knot?"

Mrinmoyee with a soft smile gently extricated her hair from Shyama's clutches.

"Well and good" continued Shyamasundari "Do but fulfil my wishes. Once attire yourself after the style of our household women. How long, Oh God, would you play the ascetic?"

"I had ever been an ascetic girl before I fell in with this son of a Brahmin."

"Now you must forego that."

"Why forego?"

"Why? would you see? I will break your asceticism. Do you know what a philosopher's stone is?"

"No"

"The philosopher's stone turns the rusty bars of iron into gold."

"What of that?"

"Women have, too, their philosopher's stone."

"What is it?"

"Man. The forest-maid with his touch blossoms into a full-blown house-wife. You have touched that stone."

Then she hummed in the following air in a tuneful voice:

> *I shall bind thy ample locks of hair*
> *And give thee shining robe to wear;*
> *Your braid shall shine with flowers fresh,*
> *A tiara shall thy temple grace;*
> *There shall be a girdle for thy waist,*
> *For ears, a pair of pendants best;*
> *Nut, leaf and betel spices sweet,*
> *Sandal and ingredients meet,*
> *Delicious shall thy cup overflow;*
> *Thy ruddy lips shall ruddier glow.*
> *There shall, a boy, as bright as gold*
> *And fair, as doll, thy arms enfold;*
> *And, I am sure, such a sight as this*
> *Will fill your heart with joy and bliss.*

"Well, now I understand. Granted, I have touched the philosopher's stone and in contact with it have turned into gold; granted, I have braided the hair and stuck up flower in the braided knot; granted, I have dangled the waist-band on the loin and hung up ear-rings in the ear; granted, I have used plenty of sandal, kunkum, chooa, betel and betel-nut and am delivered even of the precious sweet boy babe; granted, it gave a fillip to my pleasures. After all, do these make up happiness?"

"Answer if the flower has any joy in its bloom."

"Men are delighted to see it. But what does it matter to the flower?"

Shyama's looks fell and dark shadows flitted across her face. Like the petals of a lotus blown by the morning wind, her big blue eyes stared hard and twinkled.

"What has it to do with flower?" echoed she "That I can never say. I never grew up into a flower that blossomed. But if ever I could be a rose-bud like you, then perhaps I would have a taste of the thrill of delights in the blossom."

Seeing her silent, Shyama continued "Well and good. But if it does not follow, then let me hear your idea of happiness."

Mrinmoyee bethought herself a while and said "I can not explain it. Perhaps I would have been happy if I could but wander through the sea-side wilderness."

Shyamasundari was no little disconcerted to hear this. That their care and good treatment bestowed no benefits upon Mrinmoyee stung her and ruffled her temper.

"Is there any means of return?" asked she.

"No. Not any."

"Then what you propose?"

Adhicary used to say "We do as we are ordained to do."

Shyamasundari hid her face with her cloth and shook with laughter.

"As you please, your most Noble Eminence" added she. "What is the conclusion?"

Mrinmoyee heaved a heavy sigh and rejoined. "Let God's will be done. Come what may."

"What? What else in store? There are brighter and happier days for you. Why you drew that sigh?"

"Hear me," proceeded Mrinmoyee. "Just before we left the place on the day I started forth with my husband I went to place the trident leaf at Bhowani's feet as I used to undertake no work until I had done the same. The trident leaf used to stick up if the work in hand was sure to prosper and it shook and fell if the work was to end in a fiasco. I had my misgivings with regard to my adventure into a foreign land in company of a foreigner and so visited the Goddess to read the auguries. Mother Goddess let fall the trident leaf and so I am afraid what the future may bring forth."

Mrinmoyee ended. A shudder crept into Shyama and she gave a start.

PART III

I

IN THE LONG PAST

When Nabokumar left the inn with Kapalkundala, Moti also bowled off towards Burdwan along a different route. Let us have a resume of her early career so long she is on the high-way. Moti had an erratic career and her character though stained with dark vices was as well adorned with great virtues. A review of such a character may not bore the reader.

The time, her father embraced Musalman faith, her Hindu name was converted into Luthfunnisha. She never assumed the name Moti in any part of her life. But she might have had recourse to the name when she happened to travel incognito in foreign lands. Her father came to Dacca and took service under Government. The place was, however, too full of his countrymen. It ill-becomes almost every gentleman to live and move in a community wherefrom he has been black-balled. As a matter of course, when he won some feathers in his cap of success under the subadar he provided himself with credentials from many Omrahs who were his friends and made for Agra. Merits were sure to have been unearthed by Akbar and so his merits were rewarded. Luthfunnisha's father in a surprisingly short time gathered more leaves to his laurel and was reckoned as one of the most powerful Omrahs of the realm. On the other hand, Luthfunnisha was fast coming of age. On her advent into Agra, she received her lessons in Persian, Sanskrit, dance, music, wit and what not and became accomplished in all these. She was in no time looked upon as the first and foremost amongst the first-rate beauties as well as the 'blue-stockings' of the capital. As ill-luck would have it, her education was ill-grounded in religion and was not of a piece with her proficiency in other branches of knowledge. When Luthfunnisha blossomed into her glorious womanhood she showed signs of an unbridled temper. She had no control over her passions far less any inclination for it. She set her mind upon any work without arguing its pros and cons and did what pleased her. She did right when her heart took fancy for it and did wrong when it pleased her passing whim. So Luthfunnisha imbibed all the vices as the fruit of her unlicensed youthful follies. Her first husband was alive so none of the Omrahs consented to marry her. Marriage, too, had not its much attractiveness for her. She thought she found no earthly necessity in clipping short the wings of the dallying amorous bee sipping from flower to flower. The first whisperings culminated in a deep-mouthed public scandal. Her father was annoyed and she was expelled from her father's residence. The heir-apparent, Selim, was one of those upon whom her favours were bestowed in secret. Selim, however, could not make Luthfunnisha an inmate of his harem lest his actions cast a blot on the family escutcheon of an Omrah and he, himself, incurred the flaming wrath of his imperial father. Now the moment proved opportune. Selim's chief Begum was the sister of Mansinha, the Rajput chief. The prince gave Luthfunnisha the situation of the first maid-of-honour to the Begum. Luthfunnisha publicly showed, herself, as the maid to the Begum, while in secret was in liasion with the heir-apparent.

It can be easily imagined that a woman of the intellectual stamp of Luthfunnisha could shortly win the heart of the prince. She gained such an unrivalled ascendency over Selim's mind as made her cocksure that she bade fair to be Selim's prospective chief Begum at the right nioinent. Not only was Luthfunnisha cocksure about it but all the palace household thought it a possibility. Luthfunnisha bore her charmed existence under the spell of such golden dreams when one day she received a rude awakening. Meherunnisha, the daughter of Khowja Ayesh (Aktimuddaulah), Akbar's High Treasurer, held the first rank amongst Moslem beauties. The Chancellor of Exchequer one day invited Selim and other shining lights to a dinner at his residence. That day Selim saw Meherunnisha for the first time. At the first sight he lost his heart and confided his smitten soul to her care. What followed then is known to every reader of the Indian History. The High Treasurer's daughter was, before this, affianced to a powerful Omrah named Sher Afgan. Selim blinded by passion approached his father to have the engagement cancelled.

The result was that he met with a stern rebuff from his impartial father. But his ardour received a temporary set-back only. Being disarmed for sometime he did not give up the game. Though Meherunnisha was married off to Sher Afgan Luthfunnisha, however, looked through Selim's soul as if in a mirror and she knew it for certain that the fate of one thousand-fold stout-hearted Sher Afgan was sealed for ever. With the death of Akbar his life would be violently cut short and Meherunnisha would perforce be made the Begum wife of Selim.

Luthfannisha gave up the idea of the throne as a thing not worth a moment's purchase. The days of Akbar, the glory of the Moghul race of emperors, were drawing to a close. The glaring sun that shed its effulgence over the sweep of the country from the Brahmaputra to Turkistan was on its decline. Luthfunnisha at this time planned a bold coup to assert her personality.

The Begum of Selim was the sister of Mansinha, the Rajput chief and Khasru was her son. One day Luthfunnisha was conversing with her on the topic of Akbar's illness and was congratulating her on her being a Badsha's wife.

"Life's highest ambition may be attained" retorted the mother of Khasru "in the exalted position of a Badshah's wife but the mother of a Badsha is the highest of all." At this the fertile mind of astute Luthfunnisha formed a daring scheme.

"Why not let it be so?" replied she "This, too, is under your thumb."

"What is it?" asked the Begum.

"Have the kindness to bestow the throne on Khasru" archly added the sly schemer.

The Begum made no reply. No further issue was raised on the same topic on the same day but none forgot about it. That the son should sit on the throne instead of the father was not after the liking of the Begum but Selim's affection towards Meherunnisha was as much gall and wormwood to Luthfunnisha as to the Begum herself. Why she, the sister of Mansinha would brook the bondage of an upstart Turkoman's daughter? Luthfunnisha had also a deep motive to be an instigator to the scheme. The same question cropped up on a different day and the two came to a decision. It could never be canvassed an impossibility to place Khasru on Akbar's throne to the exclusion of Selim. Luthfunnisha impressed this fact on the Begum's mind.

"The Moghul empire has been won by the Rajput sword" exhorted she "and Mansinha, the maternal uncle of Khasru, is the noblest of the Rajput race. Also Khan Ajim, Khasru's father-in-law, is the Prime Minister and head of the Moslems. If the two pull together on his behalf, who would not follow the suit? On whose support else can the prince count to seize the throne? It rests on you to make Mansinha pull his whole weight into the boat and it remains with me to bring over Khan Ajim and other Mahomedan Omrahs to our side. With your benediction I am sure to succeed but the dread is lest Khasru on his accession to the throne drives this miscreant out of the Palace."

The Begum divined the lady-in-waiting's motive. A happy genial smile relaxed her expressions and she said "Any Omrah of Agra in whose household you choose to be a mistress shall accept your hand in marriage. Your husband shall be created a Manshabdar and shall command 5000 horse."

Luthfunnisha was mightily pleased. This also was her heart's choice. If she was to be an obscure harem woman in the palace what joy was there for the flirting flapper who won't come flapping any more. If she was to buy this at the cost of shackling her liberty, then what happiness could there be in her serfdom to Meherunnisha, her friend since the time they were lasses. Rather is it a thing of greater honour to be the supreme ruler of a minister's household. So this did not hold out sufficient bait to lure Luthfunnisha into the marrying business. Besides, her ruling idea was to avenge the wrong she suffered at the hands of Selim, the more so as he overlooked her claims upon his affection and hankered so much after Meherunnisha. Khan Ajim and other Omrahs of Agra and Delhi were under great obligation to Luthfannisha. So it did not appear strange that Khan Ajim would bestir himself in the interest of his son-in-law. He and the rest of the party agreed to the proposal.

"Suppose the scheme fizzles out through any inopportuneness" said Khan Ajim to Meherunnisha "then it might not offer us any chance of escape. Therefore it is meet that we should have at least some loop-holes of retreat."

"What is your advice?" asked Luthfunnisha.

"There is no shelter other than Orissa" said Khan Ajim "where the Moghal grip is not so tight. The army of Orissa should be brought under our palm anyhow. As your brother is a Manshabdar in Orissa, I shall proclaim it tomorrow that he has been wounded in a battle there. Start positively next day ostensibly to visit him and return quickly after fulfilling the mission so far you think it feasible." Luthfunnisha consented to this proposal. The reader saw her when she was journeying back from her visit to Orissa.

II

At the parting of ways

The day Moti or Luthfannisha as she was called bade farewell to Nabokumar, she started out on her journey towards Burdwan. She could not reach her destination the same day. So she stopped at a wayside inn. Towards the evening when she sat tete-a-tete with her Peshman or chamber-maid she suddenly asked "Peshman, how did you see my husband?"

Peshman was a little taken aback at the abrupt question and replied "What to see other than a plain man?"

"If he is not a handsome person?" interrogated Moti again.

Peshman developed a great aversion for Nabokumar. She had an eye on the ornaments Moti gave away to Nabokumar and was anxiously looking forward to the day when she would get the same on her mere asking for them. That hope was blighted now. So she came to hate both Kapalkundala and her husband. Accordingly on her mistress questioning her on the subject she retorted, "Gainly or ungainly is all the same for a poor Brahmin."

Moti took in the significance of the maid's observation and hilariously said "If the poor Brahmin blossoms into an Omrah whether he would not look all the more handsome?"

"What a new idea?"

"Why? Don't you remember the Begum's promise that my husband shall be created an Omrah when Khasru becomes the Badsha?"

Know it I do, of course. But what earthly reason is there that your former husband shall be made an Omrah?"

"Besides, what other husband have I got?"

"I mean the prospective new husband"

Moti jestfully added "It is a wicked thing for a chaste woman like me to be in possession of two husbands!—who goes there?"

Peshman happened to recognise the man, whom Moti challenged, to be a creature of Khan Ajim of Agra. Both looked flurried. Peshman called in the man who came forward, saluted Luthfunnisha and handed in a letter to her. Moreover, he said "I was carrying the letter to Orissa because of its urgency."

The reading of the missive gave a death-blow to Moti's high hopes and cherished aspirations of life. The letter ran as follows:—

"Our energies are of no avail. Even on death-bed Akbar Shah defeated our ends by his art and sagacity. His soul has passed away into eternity. Under his orders Prince Selim has assumed the title of Jehangir Shah. You need not worry yourself about Khasru. Come back posthaste with a view to baffle any design of hostility towards you on the occasion."

The way Akbar Shah broke up the conspiracy is described in history. So it is out of place to give an account here.

When the messenger was sent away with a reward, Moti read out the letter to Peshman.

"Good Heavens! Any means now?" exclaimed Peshman.

"Every thing has gone by board now."

Peshman. (Thoughtfully) "But what a harm can there be? You shall be as you had been. The inmate of a Badsha's harem is far more powerful than the sovereign queen of any other land."

(With a slight laugh) "That can never be a possibility any longer. I can not live any more in the Palace as Meherunnisha shall be married to Jehangir in a short time. I know Meherunnisha from her nursery days and once she is an inmate of the harem, Jehangir shall be a Badshah in name. It will be an open secret to her that I once stood between her and the throne. Then what will be my condition?"

Peshman was about to burst into tears.

"Alas! what should be done then?" cried out she.

"There is one hope yet—how is Meherunnisha inclined towards Jehangir?" said Moti "As for her singleness of purpose, if she has actually set her heart upon her husband and has no affection for Jehangir, then Jehangir despite slaying one hundred Sher Afgans must fail to secure Meherunnisha. But if Meherunnisha takes a fancy to Jehangir, then everything is given up for lost."

"How are you to understand Meherunnisha's heart?" enquired Peshman.

"Is any feat impossible with Moti?" joined Moti with a smile "My friendship with Meherunnisha is as old as our childhood. I shall proceed to Burdwan tomorrow and stay with her for two days."

"Supposing Meherunnisha does not love the Badshah, what happens then?"

"I heard my father say 'Things should be done as judged on the spot by the test of circumstances.'"

Both remained silent for sometime. A thin smile curled the lips of Moti.

"What makes you laugh" interrogated Peshman.

"Some new impulses are coming" answered Moti.

"What new impulses?"

Moti did not speak that to Peshman. We, too, shall not speak that to the reader. This should be told later on.

III

In her rival's house

S her Afgan, at this time, was working under the Subadar of Bengal as the chief functionary of Burdwan and was living in that far-off station. On reaching Burdwan, Moti went straight to Sher Afgan's quarters. Sher Afgan with the whole family warmly received her and made her lodge with them. Moti was much known to them since the time Sher Afgan and his wife resided in Agra. A jolly good friendship existed between her and Meherunnisha.

Eventually both played each other's rival in their game of high stakes for the throne of Delhi and the empire. Now when united together, Meherunnisha thought within herself "Who is destined to wield the first power in India? Providence knows, Selim knows and if anybody else knows it is this Luthfunnisha. Let me see if she gives me to understand a bit of her mind. Moti, too, had a mind to gauge Meherunnisha's feelings.

Meherunnisha at that time won a celebrity as the first in beauty and talent in India. As a matter of fact, a woman of her calibre is such a rarity in this world. It is an admitted fact with every historian that she stands out pre-eminent in the historical group of celebrated beauties. Scarcely any even among contemporary men could hold his own with or excel her in either artistry or knowledge whatsoever. Meherunnisha was unsurpassed in dance and music and had the added charms of her skill in painting and verse-writing. Her wit had a greater fascination than her beauty. Moti, too, was no lesser an ability. These two witches set their wits today to know each other's minds. Meherunnisha was at her easel with paint and brush in her private appartments with Moti chewing betel, looking over Meherunnisha's shoulder and poring over the drawing.

"How do you judge the drawing?" asked Meherunnisha.

"It is what your painting always looks like" replied Moti. "It is a regret that no one is as much finished an artist as you are."

"Even if it be the fact, what causes the regret?"

"If any one else could have your painting skill then the likeness of your face might have been preserved."

"The entombing earth shall preserve the impress of my face." Meherunnisha made this remark in a somewhat serious air.

"Sister, what makes you awfully of a bad humour today?"

"Where is the lack of humour? But how can I forget even the thought of your leaving me tomorrow morning? Why should I not have the added pleasure of your few day's extended stay?"

"Who lacks the taste for pleasure! If it be in my power, why do I leave you? But I am other's subordinate how can I stay further?"

"You have only the ashes of your former affection left for me. Otherwise you could have remained anyhow. When you have come, why can't you lengthen the stay?"

"I have had my say. My brother is a Manshabdar in the Moghul Army. He was severely wounded in an engagement with the Pathans in Orissa and his life was in jeopardy. I had heard the unwelcome news and with the Begum's permission came out on a visit to him. I delayed much in Orissa and it ill-behoves me to delay any longer. I did not see you for long so I came and spent a few days with you."

"What is the approximate date you gave the Begum in your time-table to reach back?"

Moti understood it to be the tanut flung out by Meherunnisha. She was no match for Meherunnisha in tilting polished and pointed home thrusts. However, she did not blanch at the banter and stood her ground well.

"Is it possible to fix an exact date in a three month's return journey?" replied Moti. "I am already belated and any more delay may cause displeasure."

"Whose displeasure you risk?—Prince's or his chief Begum's!" added Meherunnisha with her world-bewitching smile.

"Why do you shame this shameless woman" rejoined Moti with a little confusion "I may incur the displeasure of both."

"But may I ask the reason why you don't publicly assume the role of the Begum? I heard that Prince Selim shall marry you and make you his beloved Begum. When does it come off?"

"I am always at other's command. Why am I to forego the little liberty I have? As a maid to the Begum I came out to Orissa but as the Begum of Selim I could never visit Orissa."

"What urgency can there be for the prospective Begum of the Delhi Emperor to come out to Orissa?"

"I can never boast that I am in the running for the chief Begumship of the Delhi Emperor. None but Meherunnisha alone is worthy enough to be the deserving consort to the Delhi Lord in this wide land of Hindustan."

Meherunnisha hung down her head.

"Sister, I can never persuade myself that you made the remark either to offened me or to probe my heart" added she after a brief respite "But I beg of you, when you speak, never to lose sight of the fact that I am the married wife of Sher Afgan—nay, the whole-heartedly ever faithful bond-slave to Sher Afgan."

Brazen Moti took the reproof with a good grace as it rather gave her the opportunity.

"I know it for certain that you are a devoted wife" urged Moti "and on that score I ventured to broach the subject before you under some pretext. My object is simply to let you know that Selim has not forgotten the glamour of your charms as yet. Beware."

"Now the whole thing has cleared up. But what do I care?"

"Fear of widowhood" put in Moti after a little hesitation.

With these words did Moti look hard and steady in the face of Meherunnisha but failed to detect any trace be-speaking either joy or terror.

Meherunnisha took up the cue and joined in a high tone of bold hauteur "Fear of widowhood! Sher Afgan is not too weak to defend himself. The more so as in the empire of Akbar the son even can not murder an innocent man with impunity."

"Of course! But the recent despatches from Agra advise that Akbar Shah died and Selim has ascended the throne. Who now shall curb the Delhi Lord?"

Meherunnisha heard not a syllable more. Her whole frame shook and quivered. She again dropped down her head and a flood of tears streamed down from her eyes.

"What makes you weep?" enquired Moti.

Meherunnisha gave a sigh and vented her feelings. "Selim is installed on the throne of Delhi but where am I?"

It served Moti's purpose. "Have you not wiped off the Prince's image as yet from your heart?" added she.

Meherunnisha felt a lump coming to her throat and she groaned "Whom shall I forget? I can forget my ownself rather than forget the Prince. But look here, sister, you have been all at once let into the secret of my heart and you must swear on oath that you shall not breathe a syllable of it into other's ears."

"Good. Your wishes shall be respected" said Moti. "But when Selim will hear that I came to Burdwan and enquire what you said about him what answer shall I make?"

Meherunnisha mused a little and then replied as an after-thought "Tell this that Meherunnisha shall worship him in her heart of hearts and, if needed, shall sacrifice herself in his interest. But she can never dishonour herself and shall always stand up for her rights and dignity. So long her husband is alive she will never show her face to the Lord of Delhi. Besides, if her husband is killed by the Emperor's own hand then there can never be the chance any more of her union with her husband's murderer on this side of the grave."

After this peroration, Meherunnisha rose on her legs and left the place. Moti was electrified at this revelation. But it was she who scored the success. Moti caught Meherunnisha tripping though the latter could not have an inkling of the hopes and aspirations that surged in the mind of the former. She who by her own resourcefulness afterwards won the overlordship over the Lord of Delhi now admitted the defeat. The reason is Meherunnisha bubbled with love and affection while Moti was a self-seeking adventuress. Moti knew perfectly well the strange composition of human heart. Her conclusion on the premises supplied by Meherunnisha proved too true afterwards. She gained by the conviction that Meherunnisha bore no tinsel affection for Jehangir. So despite her bold front and fierce talk, her frigidity was sure to thaw one day when the time struck. The Emperor, if needs he, would perforce gain his objective.

Moti's hopes and disires were all blasted at this decision. But did this make her cross-grained all the more? Far from this. Rather she felt some jubilation. Whence this unnatural pleasurable feeling came Moti failed to realise first. She started out and moved along the road to Agra. Few days were spent on the journey and in these few days she understood the mood of her mind. She dimly awakened to the glimmerings of her first consciousness that she was beginning to recover her soul.

IV

In the palace

M oti reached Agra. We have no more necessity of calling her Moti as the new impulse completely chastened her soul.

She was given an audience with Jehangir who as usual warmly received and questioned her on her brother's health and the comforts of her journey. What Luthfunnisha had told Meherunnisha came out true. At the name Burdwan in the midst of other topics Jehangir enquired what Meherunnisha said about him during her two day's stay with her. Luthfunnisha with an open mind gave him a true story of Meherunnisha's affection for him. Then the Emperor dropped into a sort of blissful forgetfulness and a blank pause ensued. One or two large drops of tears rolled down from his big eyes.

"Your Majesty" broke in Luthfunnisha "the slave has carried you the happy tidings. Why no orders have issued till now for her reward?"

The Badshah smiled and joined "Dearest, your ambition is boundless."

"Your Majesty, why this charge is laid at this slave's door?"

"The Delhi Emperor has placed his body and soul at your feet and still you press for further reward!"

"Women have many desires" added Luthfunnisha laughingly.

"What more desire you have?"

"Let the royal orders be forthcoming first that the slave's prayer shall be granted."

"Provided the royal duty is not hampered."

"The Delhi Lord's work can never suffer on the score of a single poor soul."

"Then I agree. Now let me hear the proposition."

"I have a mind to marry."

Jehangir burst into a salvo of laughter.

"This is a novel sort of desire" said he. "Has the negotiation ended in a compact anywhere?"

"Yes. Only the royal assent is wanting. No contract is valid without the royal warrant."

"What is the use of my permission? Whom you mean to help afloat in the ocean of bliss?"

"Because the slave has served her Emperor she can never be held unchaste. The slave craves permission to marry her own husband."

"Indeed! What would be the fate of this old slave then?"

"He shall be left to the care of Meherunnisha, the prospective mistress of Delhi."

"Who is this Delhi mistress Meherunnisha?"

"She who is in the running."

Jehangir thought that Luthfunnisha must have been boldly confident that Meherunnisha was the Empress elect of Delhi. As she had quite a way to go with the chance of being jockeyed out of the objects of her ambition she wished in disgust to retire from her harem life. This feeling sorely pressed down upon Jehangir's heart and he remained silent.

"Does your Majesty veto this proposal?"

"I can not withold my assent. But where is the necessity of marrying a husband?"

"Ill-starred as I am, the husband of my first marriage sought a divorce from me. Now he shall dare not forsake His Majesty's slave-girl."

The Badshah had a jocund laugh which shortly stiffened down into a rigid expression.

"My darling, you are given a 'carte blanche'" joined he "If you have the inclination, then follow the bend of it. But why are you to leave me for good? Do the sun and moon not shine in the same firmament? Do the twin buds never flower on the same stalk?"

Luthfunnisha focussed the full glare of her large wide eyes on the Badshah and rejoined "The tiny flowers may bloom but the twin lilies can never blossom on the same stem! Why am I to remain a prickly thorn at the base of your jewelled throne?"

Luthfunnisha retired into her own apartments. She did not explain to Jehangir the cause that furnished the motive power. Jehangir was satisfied with the surface view of the question as he never cared to look a little lower down than the surface. Luthfunnisha had the heart of an adamant. The fascinating graces of the royal debonair Selim failed to entrap her mind. Marble-hearted as she was, a worm now began eating into that unimpressionable heart.

V

In her own apartments

On entering her apartments, Luthfunnisha called out to Peshman who helped in undressing her. She got out of her immensely rich gold-braided garment wrought with pearls, diamonds and rubies and said to Peshman "Take this dress."

Peshman wondered not a little. The dress was recently made to order at an enormous cost.

"Why this dress to me?" asked Peshman. "What is today's report?"

"It is re-assuring news, indeed!"

"This is but too evident. Are you relieved of Meherunnisha incubus?

"Yes, now I have no more anxiety in that quarter."

Peshman made an exhibition of great delight and said "Then I count a maid to the Begum."

"If you want to be the Begum's maid then I shall speak to Meherunnisha about that."

"Why? You say that Meherunnisha is out of the running for the Badsha's Begumship."

"I never spoke that sort of stuff. What I said is I have no more anxiety on that head."

"Why no more anxiety?" snarled Peshman crossly "Everything is thrown overboard if you fail to be the Delhi mistress."

"I must cut off all connections with Agra."

"Why? Alack! I am too much a goose to grasp the situation. Let me have a full significance of today's happy tidings."

"The joyful news is that I leave Agra for good."

"Where do you go then?"

"I shall move down and settle in Bengal. If I can, I shall marry a gentleman."

"What a huge joke! I simply shudder at the idea."

"I don't jest. But I am, in all earnest, quitting Agra and have said an revoir to the Badshah."

"What an evil idea has possessed you?"

"Not an evil idea, to be sure! I sauntered through the prime of my life in Agra but what is the result? The thirst for pleasure grew into a passion with me since my childhood. To slake the thirst I left Bengal and came up here. What treasures did I not sacrifice to purchase the trash?—what dark and shady tricks did I stick at?—what ends I strove for were not encompassed? I had a surfeit of all these—wealth, power, glory, fame. But what did these lead to? Sitting, this day here, I can make a mental reckoning of every day as it passed out but I can make bold to say that I neither felt happy for a single day nor enjoyed unalloyed happiness for a single moment. The thirst was never quenched rather it grew and quickened. I can add to my hordes that are reckoned in millions and amass greater fortunes for the mere striving for it. But what for? If the true happiness lay in these, I could have been happy even for a day in all this long weary period! The yearning for pleasure is like a thin mountain stream. The clear slender rivulet at first issues out from the secret spring, lies hidden in its own bowels and no body knows about it. It bubbles and gurgles and no body hears it. On it courses down, the volume increases and the muddier it grows. This does not exhaust the whole story. Sometimes, again, the wind blows, lashes angry waves, and, sharks, crocodiles and other sea-monsters make their home therein. Farther the size grows, the water becomes all the more muddy and it tastes brine. Myriads of desolate dreary islets spring into existence in the river channel, the movement becomes sluggish and then the body of the river with all the mud and dirt loses itself into the wide deep ocean where who can say?"

"This too passes my wit. What makes the reason that all this palls upon your senses?

This puzzle why I have grown up blase has been solved at last. The pleasure I experienced though for a single night on my way back from Orissa, by far and away, out-measures the giddy round of pleasures, I tasted at a three year's stretch, under the shadow of the palace. This is the key to the problem."

"What is the explanation?"

"I looked so long like the Hindu idol. The get-up is of gold and jewel though the interior is hewn out of the hard stone. For the sake of my sense-pleasures I sported with fire though I touched not the flame. Now let me see if I can seek out a full-blooded vein in the heart of the granite."

"This, too, is all an unintelligible jargon to me."

"Have I ever loved any one in Agra?

(In an undertone) "None?"

"Then what am I if not a stone?"

"If you now be pleased to bestow your heart on any one why don't you do so?"

"This, too, is in my mind. That is why I am bent upon quitting Agra."

"What necessity is there of doing things like that? Is there none to woo in Agra that you will go down into the land of savages? Why not set your heart on the man who now loves you? What a greater lord is there on the earth than the Delhi Emperor in grace, in wealth, in power and all else besides?"

"Why does water run down the lower incline despite the sun and moon's gravitation?"

"Why?"

"It is the scroll of fate!"

Luthfunnisha did not open out her whole mind. The fire entered into the marble soul and was dissolving it into fluid.

VI

DOWN AT THE FEET

When the seed is sown in the soil, it germinates of itself. As the sprout shoots up, no body cares to know and see it. But once the seed is strewn, it sends its roots into the ground and bursts into a shaft of sprout which forces its way upward independent of the human agency. Today the plant's growth is but of a few inches and no body cares to look upon it. It grows up by degrees. Gradually the shooting sprout increases and it measures half a cubit, one cubit and so on up through all scales of progressive increase. Still if it lacks any body's interest then no body casts his eyes upon it. The days roll into month and months lapse into year when it attracts men's eyes. There can no more be the talk of inattention any longer. By degrees the tree grows and its shadow destroys other trees, or, it might be, it favours the growth of weeds and tares.

Luthfunnisha's love had a similar developement. One day, all on a sudden, did she come across the man after her fancy when she had hardly the consciousness of the first birth of the tender sentment. But the sprout burst into a rank life at that very instant. Afterwards she had no other occasion of meeting him. But in his absence, she had occasional peeps into his face from her minds' eye and enjoyed a sensuous pleasure in indulging the reminiscences which were dyed deep on her heart's tablet. The seed burst into a green sprout. The nebulous affection took colour and form. The nature of thought is to move along worn-out grooves which are the lines of least resistance until the work by its frequency develops into a habit. Luthfunnisha had always this beautiful penumbra before her mind's eye. She developed strong desires for an interview and the flow of kindred passions and inclinations grew violent pari passu. The bigger thought of the Delhi throne grew small before it. The throne appeared to have been surrounded by flames set alight by Cupid's arrows. The ideas of throne, capital and the empire were knocked on the head and she hastened down to have a look at the object of her hearts' desire. For this Luthfunnisha did not feel sick at heart at Mehernunisha's words and thoughts at which her high ambition and splendid enthusiasm went up into thin air. For this, on her return to Agra, she gave not an ounce of thought to safeguard her interests and for this she took her farewell leave of the Badshah.

Luthfunnisha reached Saptagram. She fixed her habitation in a mansion inside the town at the farthest corner from the street. All at once, the phenomenon of a splendid house thronged with troops of servants and lackeys in their brilliant uniforms of braided gold and silver burst upon the view and arrested the attention of the passers-by. Every appartment had costly furniture in it. Perfumes, perfumed waters and flower-vases with flowers on them scented the atmosphere. Furniture inlaid with gold, silver and ivory and other valuable odds and ends displayed the splendour and samptuousness. In such a gilded chamber amidst a blaze of colour and decoration sat Luthfunnisha with a dejected look with Nabokumar on a separate seat. In Saptagram Nabokumar had utmost one or two interviews with Luthfunnisha. How far was Luthfunnisha successful in her objective is given out in today's conversation."

"Then let me say good-bye" said Nabokumar after a brief silence "Don't remember me any more."

"Please do not go now" joined Luthfunnisha "Would you, if you don't mind, wait a little longer as I have not said everything I have a mind to?"

Nabokumar waited for sometime more but Luthfunnisha did not speak a word.

"Have you any thing to say?" added Nabokumar shortly after. Lutfunnisha gave no reply. She was weeping silently. On seeing her weep Nabokumar rose to his feet whereupon Luthfunnisha caught hold of the hem of his cloth. He was somewhat annoyed at this and exclaimed "Ah! What do you mean?"

"What do you want?" demanded Luthfunnisha. "Have you nothing to desire in this world? I shall give you wealth, honour, love, wit, mirth and jollity and everything else that make up happiness on this earth without wishing a return for the same. What I wish is simply to be a servant-maid to you. I don't long for the glorious position of a wife but the mere situation of a house-maid."

"I am a poor Brahmin and shall always remain a poor Brahmin" protested Nabokumar with vehemence. "I shall never stand the ugly name of a Javan woman's favourite by accepting the gift of your proferred wealth and property."

A Javan woman's secret lover! Nabokumar did not know yet that the woman was his married wife. Luthfunnisha sank down crestfallen when Nabokumar extricated the cloth-end from her grasp.

Luthfunnisha again clutched the hem of his cloth and said, "Well, let that pass. If it so ordained, I shall tear out my heart-strings and fling them into fire. I don't crave anything more than that you would fain pass this way at odd intervals, look up as towards a house-maid, and my eyes shall be feasted on the sight."

"You are a Javon woman—a second man's wife and a guilt shall be fastened upon me by such an intimacy with you. This is the last of such meetings between you and me."

A brief silence ensued. A tempest was raging in Lutfunnisha's heart. She sat motionless like a statue carved in marble. She let go the cloth-end of Nabokumar and said "Walk out."

Nabokumar walked forward and had advanced three or four steps when, all on a sudden, Luthfunnisha like a tree blown off by a tornado threw herself at Nabokumars' feet. She clasped the feet with both her hands and piteously cried out "Stone-hearted, I renounced the throne of Agra for your sake. You must not leave me."

"Go back to Agra again and give up the hope on me" said Nabokumar emphatically.

"Not in this life."

Luthfunnisha stood up straight like a bolt and haughtily said "I will never abandon your hope in this life." Drawing up to her full height, she slightly bent her swan neck and fixing the big steadfast eyes on Nabokumar's face threw herself in the right royal style. That fire of inflexible hauteur that grew less under the soft mellowed warmth of her heart's flame again flared up—that invincible iron-will that daunted not at the attempt at grasping the sceptre of the Empire of Hindustan—that indomitable energy again quickened up the feeble framework of her love-smitten soul. The nerves swelled out on her forehead and drew out a fine tracery. The bright eyes shone like the glassy sea lighted up by a brilliant sun. The nostrils dilated and throbbed. As the goose sporting along the current straightens up its neck and throws out its head threatening men and things blocking its way—as the down-trodden serpent stands erect spreading out its hood—so this furious Javan woman proudly stood up towering her head in an imperious air.

"Not in this life—you shall be made mine" exclaimed she in her rich ringing voice.

Nabokumar was terror-stricken at gazing upon this angry serpent-like form. The glory of Luthfunnisha's charm that spread out now had never before been eyed by Nabokumar. That beauty had the fatal fascination of the deadly lightening flash. It struch a chill into his heart. Nabokumar was about to walk out when the vision of a similar picture of haughty pose darted across his mind. Nabokumar, one day, being offended at the conduct of Padmabati, his first wife, tried to force out her ejection from the bed-chamber. The twelve year girl similarly wheeled round facing him with a bold look of defiance, similarly her eyes burnt, similarly her nostrils expanded and vibrated and similarly her head leaned back in a fine throw. That figure was a past memory. It now flashed in upon his mind and the parity at once struch him. Nabokumar had the shadow of a suspicion and he in a hesitatingly soft voice enquired "Who are you?"

The eye-balls of the Javan woman expanded to a greater extent and she replied "I am Padmabati."

Without waiting for the answer, Luthfunnisha hurried away from the scene. Nabokumar, too, being a bit frightened, wended his way home, his brain busy with thoughts.

VII

ON THE OUTSKIRT OF THE CITY

Luthfunnisha entered another chamber and closed the door. For full two days she cloistered herself inside the room. In these two days she determined the course she would follow. She arrived at a conclusion and set her mind upon it. The sun went low. Luthfunnisha began preparing her toilet with Peshman's help. It was a strange toilet as it had no evidence of a female make-up. She looked up the dress in the mirror and asked "How now, Peshman? Do you recognise me?"

"Impossible."

"Let me start then. See neither man nor maid follows me."

Peshman timorously added "If you pardon your slave, then she may ask one thing."

"What?"

"What is your object?"

"Final separation between Kapalkundala and her husband for the present. He shall be made mine afterwards."

"Would your ladyship just think over the project in its every possible light?—the dense jungle—the approaching night—and your lonely position?

But, without a word whatsoever, Luthfunnisha tripped forth silently. She directed her steps towards the lonely wooded outskirt of Saptagram wherein Nabokumar lived. Night had come ere she reached the place. The reader may have some recollection of the thicket which lay at a short distance from Nabokumar's dwelling place. When she gained the skirt of the forest-belt, she sat herself down beneath a tree. She sat on there for a considerable length of time, meditating the adventure She was embarking upon. Chance, however, brought her some fortuitious help.

Luthfunnisha could hear from her seat under the tree a dull continuous murmur that was maintained in its uniform key and seemed to issue from human throat. She started to her feet, looked about and saw shafts of light that cut the darkness of the wood. Luthfunnisha could outmatch a man in boldness so she guided her legs towards the place where the light burnt. First she reconnoitered the ground from behind the tree and observed that the light that shone was but the flame of the sacrificial fire and the voice she heard was the sound of incantation. She distinguished a sound in the midst of chants which she deciphered to be a name. At the mention of the name Luthfunnisha approached the man who was feeding the sacrificial fire and seated herself in proximity to him.

Let her be seated there for the present. But as the reader has not heard of Kapalkundala, for a long time, we must needs enquire her "goings on."

PART IV

I

IN BED-CHAMBER

It took Luthfunnisha almost a year to complete her return journey to Agra and thence to move down to Saptagram where Kapalkundala lived over a year as Nabokumar's wife. The same evening, when Luthfunnisha was out on her excursion amidst the wood, Kapalkundala sat in her bed-room in an abstracted mood of mind. She was not the self-same Kapalkundala whom the reader saw on the sea-beach, unadorned, with her loose curls flowing down her waist. The prophecy of Shyamasundari has materialised and the hermit girl with the touch of the philosopher's stone has bloomed into a full-fledged housewife.

Now the mass of her raven-dark hair that once hung out in heavy serpent-like coils, sweeping down her waist-line, has been gathered up and twisted in a massive knot that perched high on the back of her head. The braiding of locks even was worked up into an elaborate art-work and the fine skilled designs and figures displayed in the pleating spoke highly of Shyamasundari's finished style of hair-dressing. Every detail was faithfully attended to. Even the chaplet of flowers that encircled, like a coronet, the base of her braided coil, was not lost sight of. The unbraided locks of loose hair maintained not a uniform level of height on the crown of her head because of their crispness. So these ringlets showed themselves in small dark waves on the surface. The face is no longer half-concealed amidst her thick folds of hair. Rather it shone out bright and radiant. Only at places, the loosened stray locks caked on to parts bedewed with moisture. The skin displayed the same colour—the silver grey of a half-moon. Now gold ear-rings suspended from her ears and a gold necklace hung round her neck. The brightness of the gold rather than paling before the lustre of the skin gained in effect like the night-flowers adding to the charms of the sweet earth bathed in a flood of the weird mellow light of a quarter moon. The figure was draped in a piece of white cloth which appeared a milky cloud sailing in the silvery sky flooded with the splendours of a glorious moon. The skin showed the same gleam of moon-shine though it looked to have acquired a darker tinge than before like a speck of black cloud gathering in some distant corner of the far-off horizon. Kapalkundala was not seated alone, having Shyamasundari by her side. We shall narrate a portion of the conversation passing between them to our reader.

"How long will the brother-in-law stay here?" enquired Kapalkundala.

"He leaves tomorrow evening" replied Shyamasundari. "Alas! If I could but root up the medicinal plant tonight, I would have scored a success over him in taming him into submission. But what indignities did I not suffer because of my last night's escapade! So how can I go out this night also?"

"Does it not yield the same effect, if pulled out, at daytime?"

"How can it be of the same virtue if up-rooted during day-light hours? It must be taken out just at midnight, in loose hair, if it is to have any efficacy at all. Well, sister, that cherished hope of my heart shall never have its realisation."

"Right. I have myself seen the plant at day-time, today, and have, besides, seen the jungle it grows in. You must needs make no stirring tonight. I alone would bring you the plant."

"Our mind is not a clean slate, so we must take stock of our experience. What has happened one day may not happen over again. You must not go out at night-time anymore."

"You have no reason to have any anxiety on that score. You might have heard that night-walk grew up into a habit with me since my childhood and you must bear in mind that, if it had not been the case, I would never have come into your midst, and these eyes could not have shone upon you."

"It is due to no fear that I say that. Does it behove a house-hold maid or wife to wander in wood and forest at night-time? When we received that sharp rebuke despite our combined moves the other day, think, what it would come to, if you venture out alone at night?"

"What harm is there? Do you imagine I would count a lost character for my mere night outing?"

"I never think that way. But bad people may badly speak of you."

"Let them say as they like. The taint shall never touch me."

"We can't pass things to drift that way, as any ill-talk about you, will cut us to the quick."

"Let not yourselves be so touchy."

"I can stand even that much. But why should you make my brother unhappy?"

Kapalkundala cast a significant glance of her big bright eyes towards Shyamasundari and said "If it destroys his peace of mind, then there is no help for it. If I could but know that wedlock is a serfdom, I would never have suffered myself to be led to the marriage altar then!"

What followed then grew distasteful to Shyamasundari. So she left the place and went about her own work. Kapalkundala, as well, busied herself in doing the daily round of her household duties. Having finished her day-work, she left the house in quest of the drug. The first watch of the night passed away. It was moonlight then. Nabokumar was seated in a room in the front wing of his house, so he could clearly see, through the window-bars, Kapalkundala steal away from it. No sooner he saw this than he went out and, going forward at quick step, grasped her by her arm. Mrinmoyee turned back and questioned "What is the matter?"

"Where are you going" asked Nabokumar. He had not the slightest ring of reproof in his voice.

"Shyamasundari wants to charm her husband," replied Kapalkundala "so I am going to search the drug."

"Good" added Nabokumar in his former silky voice. "You had already been out overnight. What is the use of going over again tonight?"

"I could not find it out last night. So I would essay my second try this time."

"Very well," said Nabokumar in his blandest tone "You might as well conduct the search at day-time." His voice was full of pathos.

"The day-light finding won't give the desired effect" rejoined Kapalkundala.

"What necessity is there for your drug-searching? Just tell me the name of the plant and I shall bring you the thing."

"I know the plant but do not know the name. Besides, if you root it up, it won't serve the purpose. It is for women to pull it out in loose hair. So you should not put a spoke into other's wheel." Kapalkundala had a tone of displeasure in her words.

Nabokumar made no further objection and added "Move on. I shall accompany you."

Kapalkundala with a touch of swagger replied "Come and see with your own eyes if I hold not the plighted troth."

Nabokumar could not speak a word more. With a sigh he dropped down Kapalkundala's hand and got back home. Kapalkundala alone went on her way and entered the wood.

II

In the wood

A little mention has been made before of the wooded character of this side of Saptagram. A thick forest lay at a short distance from the village. Kapalkundala wended along a narrow sylvan alley to hunt out the drug. The night was sweet and cool and an unearthly stillness hung in the air. In the vernal nightsky was the cold shining moon cleaving her way silently athwart the fleecy clouds. The forest trees and creepers were shimmering noiselessly in the cold moonlight on the earth below. Smoothly did tree-leaves reflect the moon-beam and softly did milk-white flowers put forth their blossoms inside the shrubs and foliage. The whole country-side was bathed in a gracious peace. The atmospheric closeness was hardly punctuated with the occasional wing-flutter of birds disturbed in their night-roosts—with the crackle of a dead leaf falling down on the earth—with the whish of the serpent kind crawling amidst dry leaves lying about underneath—and with the faint barking of some night dogs at a far-off distance. It was not that no wind was blowing—it was the soft, refreshing, rippling breath of the spring. It was as much soft and silent as shook the top-leaves of trees, tossed the green verdure and foliage bowing down to the earth, and drifted the broken vapoury clouds scudding along the deep blue nightsky. The soft touch of that gentle sigh of wind was only awakening in one's mind the reminiscences of the past happiness experienced with such an association.

The remembrance of Kapalkundala slowly and gradually flew back to her jolly good old days and was reviving the past with all its realism. She remembered the surf-touched cool sea-breeze that playfully shook her dishevelled hair on the sand-dunes of the Bahari. She gazed into the unrelenting blue of the sky and recollection brought back to her mind the cameo-cut impressions of the boundless stretch of the sea resembling the vast deep azure of the sky overhead. With a heart heavy with such reflections did Kapalkundala walk onward.

In her distracted mood of mind she never gave a thought either to the object of her mind or the scene of her action. The track she was following proved gradually impassable. The forest grew denser and the moon-beam was almost entirely intercepted by the thickly interlaced branches and leaves making an archway above until by degrees the narrow pathway was blotted out from her eyes. Through the uncertainty of the forest-path, Kapalkundala awoke from her deep reverie and the real conception of the truth was burnt into her soul. She cast up her eyes on all sides and saw a light burning in the distant reaches of that thicket. Luthfunnisha, too, had similarly observed this glow of light before. Kapalkundala, as a result of her past habits, was always bold and on the tip-toe of curiosity on such occasions. So she slowly headed towards the glimmering light. No body could be found there where the fire was glowing. But at a few yard's distance stood a dilapidated house which was invisible from a distance on account of the forest shadows.

The house, though brick-built, was very mean and ordinary, and consisted of one room only. The sound of hushed human voices was heard issuing from it. Kapalkundala with cat-like paces approached the outer wall and, no sooner she gained it, than it appeared two men were conversing in whisper. At first she could not make out any meaning from the indistinct words but, afterwards, her repeated efforts set an edge on her hearing and she read the following conversation.

"Death is my objective" said one voice "But in case, you don't agree, I can't bring myself to help you. I also don't want any assistance from you in the fulfilment of my design."

"I, too, never count a well-wisher" replied the other voice. "But I wish her rather to be sacked and packed off, for good, to some distant place than to be myself an abettor in her murder. On the other hand, I shall oppose the act."

"Thou art foolish and insensate," joined the first voice "so I must impart some wisdom to you. Now give me your undivided attention as I shall unfold some deep-hidden secret. Meanwhile, go out and have a searching glance, all around, as I seem to hear human respiration."

As a matter of fact, Kapalkundala stood almost in touch with the house-wall, posing her fine head intently to catch the faint sound inside and breathed deep and hard like a tiny pair of bellows out of white-hot eagerness and terror.

At the companion's behest, one of the plotters came out and at once perceived Kapalkundala who also distinctly saw the person's contour and lineaments in the clear moon-light in the glade. Hardly could she make out whether her spirit lifted or fell at the sight. She found the stranger in Brahmin-garb—in dhoti—and the exterior well-covered under a muslin. The Brahmin looked of tender age with the down of youth hardly visible on the upper lip. The face was exceedingly beautiful—as beautiful as that of a woman—but unlike women it was full of glowing spirit and pride. The hair, quite unusual with men showed no sign of a razor's touch and being unclipped, as with women, crowded upon the muslin and be-spread the back, the shoulder, the arm and, least of all, the bosom. The forehead was broad and high, though a bit swollen with a solitary vein showing out in the middle—the eyes full of brilliance as of lightning flashes—and a long drawn sword in the hand. But amidst all this colouring, gleamed a spectre of frightfulness, as if, a black gaunt shadow of a dark, sinister design lent its pigment to the lustrous gold of the skin. The glance, keen as a knife-blade, cut into Kapalkundala's heart. Both stared on at each other's face for sometime. Kapalkundala was the first to flutter her eyelids and, with the first flutter, the stranger asked "Who are you?"

If a year ago, the same question would have been put to Kapalkundala in the forest of Hijli, then her response would have been quick and pertinent. But she now partook of the character of a gentle-born house-wife. So she could not make any immediate rejoinder.

The Brahmin-looking person seeing Kapalkundala demur added in a grave tone "Kapalkundala, what has brought you to this deep part of the forest in this dead of night?"

She was in wild stupefaction to hear her name on the lips of an unknown night-walker and looked a bit scared. So no instantaneous reply issued from her lips.

"Have you heard the conversation passing between us?" querried the Brahmin-attired person again.

All on a sudden did Kapalkundaia regain her lost speech.

"I, too, am asking you the same question" said she without answering the querry. "What a dark plot were you two hatching at this depth of night in this depth of forest?"

The man with the Brahmin's appearance remained mute and silent, for a short while, his mind lost in thoughts. Suddenly, a new scheme seemed to evolve itself in his mind congenial to his purpose. He advanced and grasped Kapalkundala's arm and under his firm grip led off her to a place, a little removed from the dilapidated house. But Kapalkundala, indignantly, tore herself away from his clutch when the Brahmin-guised man brought his mouth near Kapalkundala's ear and spoke in a soft undertone "Have no fear. I am not a man."

Kapalkundala was all the more startled at this. She partly believed the words though the words could not carry their full weight with her. She followed the person in Brahmin's habit and when the two reached a spot from where the house was lost to sight, the latter whispered into the former's ear "Do you want to hear what a yarn we were spinning? It concerned you only."

This whetted Kapalkundala's eagerness and she said "Yes."

"Wait here till I return" joined the other.

Then the sham Brahmin retraced his steps towards the ruined house while Kapalkundala was left seated there alone. But what she saw and heard excited some fear within her. While seated alone in the dark deep forest, her anxiety waxed intensified. Because, who could divine the motive why the false man left her seated there alone? Might be, she was kept there waiting to give the masqueraded Brahmin the facility for the execution of his dark sinister design! On the other hand the disguised Brahmin was overdue to re-enter his appearance. So Kapalkundala could not wait any longer. She rose to her feet and quickened her steps to get back home.

At that time black rolling clouds gathered in the horizon. The lowering sky took on a leaden hue that drew its drab lines across everything. The insufficient light that struggled into the wood through the interstices of luxuriant foliage grew smaller and it could scarcely direct Kapalkundala on to the track. So she could not tarry a moment longer. She went her way back in hurried steps in order to issue out of the forest. While on the retreat, she thought she heard a second man's foot-falls behind. But on looking back, her eyes could not peer through the thick cloak of gathering gloom. She believed the Brahmin-garbed person to have been dogging her steps. So she left the forest-belt and re-entered the previously spoken wood-path. The place was less dark here and so a man happening to be in the line of vision was sure to be discerned. But so far nothing was visible. Accordingly she acclerated her speed. But again the shadowing footsteps distinctly struck her ear. The sky was thickly overcast and the dark grey thunder-clouds looked all the more threatening. Kapalkundala threw in an extra ounce of energy into her gait. Before the gleam of the house-top sticking across the ground met her eyes, the storm burst with the savage snarl of a tornado and rain began in torrents. Kapalkundala dashed forward. She guessed from the footsteps behind that the other man also ran. The thunder-storm had pursued its mad career over her head, before she reached the doorstep. Thunder clapped and the air vibrated with the crash of terrific electric discharges. The sky opened sheets of flame that played in zigzag way and the rain continued its pourings. Saving her skin anyhow, Kapalkundala regained her homestead. She bounded across the yard and lightly jumped on to the house-terrace. The door of the room stood ajar, so she burst inside. No sooner she wheeled her back, facing the inner-yard, to close the door, than it appeared she saw a big burly man standing at the centre of the quadrangle. At this moment, the lightning flashed once for all and under the solitary gleam of that light she recognised the man. The man was no other than the former Kapalik who dwelt upon the lonely sea-shore.

III

In dream

Slowly and silently Kapalkundala closed the door—slowly and silently she crept into the bedroom—and slowly and noiselessly she laid herself down on the bed-stead. Man's mind is like a boundless ocean. What man is there who can count the tumbling, rollicking waves that are whipped into fury by the storm and wind raging across its breast? Who could reckon, then, the endless waves that tossed and swelled on the storm-swept ocean-like mind of Kapalkundala?

Nabokumar did not come into the inner-appartments that night through heart-sickness. So Kapalkundala lay alone in her bed-room though sleep did never visit her eyes. She seemed to see around her, in the midst of darkness, that terrible face, surmounted by a crown of matted locks tossed up by the high wind and drenched in the rain that dribbled from it. Her mind retrospected the past events, chapter by chapter, as they happened, and dangled before her vision, the slovenly treatment she accorded to the Kapalik on the eve of her departure—the fiendish acts he used to perpetrate in the sea-side wilderness—his Bhairobi worship—and Nabokumar's bondage and she gave an involuntary start. Her thoughts flew backward again across space and time and recalled the same night's incidents—Shyama's feverishness for the drug—Nabokumar's warning—Kapalkundala's admonition—the weird moon-light beauty in the shaded glade—the gathering gloom under the forest-trees—the chance companion in the forest purview—and the strange commingling of a shapely form with the leering spectre of horridness in him.

When the first glitter of the radiant dawn emblazoned the eastern sky, did Kapalkundala fall into a light sleep and in that short light sleep she saw dreams. It appeared she was out in a pleasure-boat on a joy-row across the bosom of the previously seen ocean. The boat was gaily dressed with bunting, and pennons of gold and yellow flew from the peak, bow and port. The oarsmen rowed merrily with flower garlands festooned round their necks and sang jolly tunes of the amorous ditties of Radha Shyam. The sun was raining down liquid gold from the western sky and under the sunny shower of that golden cascade the sea smiled and gaily rippled by. Clouds scudded along the sky steeped and refreshed in the riotous profusion of the sparkling light and colour. In the midst of such simpering mirth and rollicking jollity, the sun suddenly went out and night came up. Dark blue clouds mantled the sky and everything was kicked up into confusion. The crew turned the head of the boat though they knew not which way to steer her as the compass lost its bearings. They stopped singing and tore through the flower garlands. Flags of yellow and gold were rent through and the flag-staff crashed overboard. Wind rose, mountain-high waves leapt into fury, and out of this tumult of elements, a bulky man of matted locks came forward and, seizing one side of Kapalkundala's boat, was about to hurl her into the mid-ocean. At this psychological moment, the same person of graceful mien tinged with a grim humour depicted on every line of the face and dressed in a Brahmin's guise appeared on the scene and held fast the boat.

"Whether I shall rescue or drown you" asked he.

"Drown me" issued from the lips of Kapalkundala.

The seeming Brahmin gave a shove to the boat and the boat got her voice and spoke "I can't carry this load any further. Let me go deep down into the bowels of the earth."

With these words, the boat flung away Kapalkundala into water and went down into the pit far into the earth below.

Dripping in perspiration, Kapalkundala startled out of her dream and rubbed her eyes. It was dawn and the window stood wide open. Puffs of balmy, soft spring breeze came stealing into the room through the window bars. Wild birds of the wood were singing their joyous carols amidst tree-branches rocked by the wind. Sundry lovely wood trailers laden with sweet-scented flowers traced a natural trellies-work around the window casement and were gently gesticulating before it. Kapalkundala, through her tender womanly nature was engaged in arranging the blossoms in a bunch and patting the blooms in places when lo! A missive came out from their midst. Kapalkundala was brought up under Adhicary's tutelage and so she learned to read. She read the contents as follows:-

"Please see the last night's Brahmin boy, after evening, tonight. You shall hear important things which you want to."

One in Brahmin's disguise.

IV

At the tryst

The same day until sundown, was Kapalkundala taken up, in thinking out the reasonableness of her meeting with the masqueraded Brahmin. She never paused over the profaneness of the thought for a faithful wife to visit, at night-time, a strange man which goes, always, without a social warrant. The basic idea of her mind was that so long there is the purity of purpose such an action can never be judged impious. The social claim of intercourse exclusively between men or women is as much a legitimate natural right as between men and women specially when the Brahmin-dressed youth is of uncertain description. So her qualms were set at rest. But whether such a meeting would produce beneficial or baneful results gave an uncertain outlook to the whole affair that made her indecisive. First, the Brahmin-like boy's conversation, then the Kakalik's appearance and, lastly, the dream—all these conjoined to confirm her suspicion that she might have some smack of the danger that cast its shadows before. The flutter of a suspicion as to the existence of a connecting link between the advent of the Kapalik and some sort of evil-doing looked to have some substratum of truth. The young boy of a seeming Brahmin appeared to be the Kapalik's associate and the adventure of an interview might have all the risk of ensnaring her into a trap deeply laid in the plot. Did not the disguised Brahmin clearly tell her, the other day, that the conspiracy was set on foot against her alone? Besides, it can be suggestive of the beginning of the end. The man with whom the Brahmin-looking boy was in secret conversation appeared to have been the Kapalik. This is the sure indication that they were plotting, either, somebody's murder, or, transportation. Whose it might be? When she was the subject of all these secret plottings and machinations, then her death or transportation was certainly being contemplated. Come what may! Then the dream!—but what is the significance of it? In vision she saw the Brahmin-guised boy rush forward to save her in the supreme moment of crisis and the dream now looks to have all the appearance of a reality.

"Drown me" said she in dream to the masqueraded Brahmin. Is she to re-iterate the same in actuality? Oh, no! the votary-loving Bhowani graciously sent instructions for her preservation and the Brahmin-garbed youth volunteered to her rescue. Now, in case of refusing the help, she is sure to be drowned. Therefore Kapalkundala made it a point to see the young man. It is under doubt whether a sane man would have similarly concluded. But we have nothing to do with sane conclusions. Kapalkundala had no wisdom of a wise-woman and so she had not a wise woman's counsel all to herself. She came by her conclusion like a young woman eager after the curious—like a girl bewitched by a finely moulded form with a dark sinister air hanging about him—like a Sannyasi-trained girl used to rove gaily amidst wild landscapes at night—like a holy woman actuated under deep reverential feelings towards Bhowani—and like an insect on the eve of its headlong plunge into the shooting flame of a burning fire. Kapalkundala finished her household work and set out towards the forest after night-fall. She had stirred the lamp flame before she went out and the lamp burnt all the brighter. Scarcely she left the room when the light went out. She had forgot one thing before she started on her parlous errand. What could be the place the imposter of a Brahmin fixed as the meeting ground in the letter? So she came back and searched the place high and low where she put the letter. But, alas! no letter could be found there. It occured to her that in order to keep it on her person she had tucked it up in her pleated hair. Accordingly, she ran her finger nails in and around her braided knot. When her finger tips did not come across it, she unloosened her hair. However, the letter remained untraced as before. Then she rummaged every part of the house but still it could not be found. At last, when she lost every trace of it, she thought she might see him where they had met before. Due to the lack of spare moments, she could not arrange the mass of her hair. Thus, she went forth, as with her unmarried days before, her figure within her rich glorious hair that hung down, all around, in wavy curls about her.

V

On the door-step

When towards evening, Kapalkundala was engaged in doing her round of house-hold duties, the letter, loosening from its hold in the braided hair, fell on to the ground. Anyhow she was unaware of the incident. But Nabokumar saw the letter slipping down to the floor from her hair which set him wondering. When Kapalkundala was called away by some other work, he picked up the missive and read over it. The reading suggested the same conclusion "You will hear of things you, yesterday, wanted to." What is it? Is it a love affair? Is the Brahmin-looking person, the secret lover, of Mrinmoyee? The story pointed to a single moral to the man who never knew overnight's occurrence.

As when a devoted wife in practising the Suttee, or, for some other reasons, mounts her funeral pyre and sets fire to it with her own hands, then, first, the rolling volume of smoke makes a curtain all around, puts out the sight and blots out everything. Then, by degrees, the fire-logs begin to burn and crackle, the sharp tongues of flame begin to loll out from underneath and lick the body at places, and, afterwards, when the fire bursts with a terrific roar into a huge ring of flame, it envelopes the quick body and all else besides. Lastly, the leaping flames soar heavenward, enliven the horizon and reduce all and sundries to ashes.

Nabokumar had a similar taste of sensation when he finished the letter. First, he could not clearly define it, but, next moment, dark suspicion which always flutters like an owl in twilight, crossed his mind, and, finally the dim outlines took shape and form of the burning truth which left a stinging smart behind. Men's minds are so moulded that they are unable to bear extremes of pleasure and pain. First, the dense smoke and fume sorrounded Nabokumar, then, the fire set his soul alight and, lastly, the flame burnt out his heart-string. He had already marked Kapalkundala's rebelliousness in many respects. Besides, inspite of all his warnings, she always went out alone of her own free will and choice and deported irresponsibly with each and everybody. Moreover, she never cared to mind his words and would rather move about, unattended, in his nightly wanderings amidst forest and wilderness. Other people might have their suspicions, but, Nabokumar, apprehending, that once the green-eyed jealously is aroused, its torment will be as much a hellish fire as the never-quenching stinging bite of a scorpion, never harboured any distrust about the good conduct of Kapalkundala for a single day. He would never have entertained such a feeling even this day. But these were no mere doubts any longer that crystalised in unchallenged hard facts. He sat mute and alone for sometime and wept hot tears of sorrow. The free vent of tears brought him some relief and, then, he settled his line of action. He determined in his mind that he would throw up no hints to Kapalkundala, but would, rather, follow her, when in the evening, she would go out into the forest, see with his own eyes her sinful enactments and then, at last, violently cut short his own miserable existence. He would kill his ownself rather than communicating anything to Kapalkundala. What other alternative was left open to him? He was unable to muster sufficient strength to bear the fardels of humanity any longer.

Having thus made up his mind, he fixed his eyes upon the back-exit of the house on the look-out for Kapalkundala's outing. Kapalkundala, as usual, went out and after she had traversed some distance, Nabokumar also left the house and followed her. But she was seen retracing her steps again to have a look at the previously spoken lost letter whereupon Nabokumar gave her a slip. Afterwards, when Kapalkundala walked out of the house for the last time and crossed over some ground forward, did Nabokumar issue out of the back-door to do his shadowing work. Just at this moment, the outline of a big bulky man was thrown up against the doorway darkening the threshold. What that man might be and what business had he to let fall his shadow across the door-step, Nabokumar had no mind to enquire, least of all, he scarcely bestowed even a look upon him. All he bustled about was to follow Kapalkundala with his eyes. So he gave the big man a big push in his breast in order to clear his way though the big push could scarcely shove him an inch.

"What are you? Get you gone. Make room for me" burst from Nabokumar's lips.

"Who am I?" exclaimed the stranger. "Don't you know me?"

The deep bass voice had the resonance of the sea. Nabokumar looked up and saw him, his former acquaintance, the Kapalik, with a crown of matted locks trailing down on all sides. Nabokumar was startled but not frightened.

A ray of hope darted across Nabokumar's face and he, immediately, asked "Is Kapalkundala going out to see you?"

"Oh! No" answered the Kapalik.

The last ray of hope had departed before it gleamed and dark shadows flitted across Nabokumar's face.

"Don't cross my path anymore" uttered Nabokumar.

"I will let you pass" said the Kapalik "but you must hear me, first, what I shall speak to you."

"Words I have none with you" cried out Nabokumar. "Do you hover after me to take my life again? Slay me this time and I shall not any more thwart you. Now, wait here till I come back. Why did I not give up my mortal flesh to appease gods? As I have sowed so I reap now. She who preserved the sacred flame of my life is extinguishing it now. Kapalik, you must not distrust me any longer. No sooner I got back than I will surrender my body to you."

"I have looked in here" said the Kapalik "not for your annihilation as this is never the will of Bhowani. I have called at this quarter to settle some old accounts which must needs have your approval. Lead me into the house, first, and listen what I say to you."

"Not now" joined Nabokumar "I shall lend you my ears afterwards. Wait here for the present and let me come back after despatch of some urgent work."

"My son, I know everything. You are going to follow that miscreant. I know perfectly well where she will go. I will take you with me there and show you over the place. Now hear what I say and take no fright on any account."

"I have no longer any fear from you. Come along."

Then, Nabokumar took the Kapalik inside his house and gave him a small mat to sit upon. Having seated, himself near him, he said "Just begin."

VI

In conversation

Having taken his seat, the Kapalik showed Nabokumar his two hands which were broken.

The reader may remember that the same night when Nabokumar fled from the sea-shore in company of Kapalkundala, the Kapalik, in hunting down the couple, fell from the crest of a sand-hill. In course of his fall to the earth, he tried to save his body by clutching the ground with his two hands. Thus he saved his body but could not save his arms which were fractured. He narrated the whole story to Nabokumar in detail and then said "I feel not much difficulty in going through my daily necessary work though I possess no strength in them. They are of no service to me, even, in collecting dry sticks of wood."

Afterwards, he said "At the moment, I fell to the earth, I could not feel that my hands were fractured though the body was uninjured, as I swooned away at the time. First I lay in a perfect comatose state which was later on broken by half-conscious states. I have no clear recollection how long I lay in this condition but at its rough guess it might be estimated at two nights and one day. It was in the morning that I came to. Exactly before this, I had a dream. "As if Bhowani" and at this stage a shudder passed through his framework "as if Bhowani appeared in flesh and form before me and brow-beat and chid me. She then said 'Wretch, you hindered the true and right form of my worship through the uncleanliness of your soul. You did not so long worship me with this maid's blood owing to your ulterior evil purpose. So through this girl, the merits of your previous good acts will be destroyed. I shall never more accept any offerings from you'."

Then I sobbed aloud and rolled at the feet of the Mother who was then pleased to say 'Gentleborn, I prescribe the only means of atonement for you. I want you to sacrifice that Kapalkundala before me. Worship me not till you have fulfilled your mission'."

It is unnecessary to narrate here, how and when, I recovered. But, no sooner had I become a convalescent than I set about to carry out the orders of Bhowani. Then, I found that I had not a baby's strength left in my arms and that my labours can never fructify with a pair of powerless hands. So I must needs have a helpmate. But the work of religious merits is not the forte of the average people, now-a-days, the more so, in this iron age, when men do not make it their worth while to come of any service to the working out of a noble mission for fear of punishment as their acts are calculated to be judged prejudicially by the biased minds of authorities. After a prolonged search, I have discovered this wretch's habitation. But due to no strength in my arms, I could not fulfil the words of Bhowani. I am in the habit of performing my rites according to Tantrick rules in order to attain my ends. Last night, when I kept alight the sacrificial fire, I saw with my own eyes Kapalkundala, with love warm upon her, in flirtation with a young Brahmin. This evening, too, is she going out to see him. If you have a mind to look on at the scene, you can come off with me and I will show you over the place." My son, Kapalkundala is worth sacrificing. I will slay her in obedience to Bhowani's call. She has, besides, proved faithless to you, so she is punishable with death before your eyes. Give me the necessary help by seizing this miscreant and conducting her to the sacrificial ground. Slay her, therefore, with your own hand and this will wash the sin you committed before God and men. By this, you will earn religious merits of a far-reaching character—the girl accused of her marriage infidelity shall meet with her condign punishment—and, lastly, it will furnish a fitting denouement to a work of noble revenge."

The Kapalik finished his speech but Nabokumar made no reply. The Kapalik watched this muteness in Nabokumar and urged "My son, do you wish to see, now, what I promised to show you over?"

Reeking in perspiration, Nabokumar followed the Kapalik.

VII

GREETING WITH CO-WIFE

Kapalkundala, coming out of the house, entered the wood. First, she went inside the ruined house where she had met the Brahmin boy. If it would have been day-light, she could have seen the pallor on his face. The made-up Brahmin said faintly to Kapalkundala, "As the Kapalik might turn up here, we should not have any talk at this place. So, let us go somewhere else."

Amidst the greenery, was some clean space with trees on all sides and a track issuing out of it. The youth in Brahmin's attire took Kapalkundala there and, both having seated, said "Let me open my own story first. This will enable you to judge how far my words are faithfully correct. When, in company of your husband, you were coming from the Hijli side, you met with a Javan woman on the way. Do you remember that?"

Kapalkundala—"She who gave me ornaments?"

"Yes, I am she."

Kapalkundala was much astonished. Luthfunnisha marked her astonishment and said "There is reason of a greater wonder—I am your husband's co-wife." Kapalkundala was lost in wonder and cried "How is it?"

Luthfunnisha, then, recounted the full chapter of her past career, incident by incident. She spoke everything—marriage—ostracism—divorce by husband—Dacca—Agra—Jehangir—Meherunnisha—quitting of Agra—living in Saptagram—meeting with Nabokumar—Nabokumar's treatment—last night's incognito visit to the wood—and chance acquaintance with the sacrificial Brahmin. Now Kapalkundala asked "With what object did you wish to visit our house?"

"To separate you from your husband."

Kapalkundala fell into a thoughtful air and enquired "How could you gain your end?"

"At present, I would have engrafted a doubt on your husband's mind as to your fidelity. But truce to such a talk as I have forsaken that path. Now, if you follow my advice, then, through you alone I may attain my object, while at the same time, you will be benefitted."

"What name did you hear issue from the sacrificial Brahmin's throat?"

"It is yours. I bowed to him and sat down to divine his motive, good or bad, in kindling the sacrificial fire. When the ceremony ended, I asked him by trick of words, why he offered sacrifices in your name. A few minute's conversation convinced me that to harm you was the object of his sacrifice. I was, also, similarly disposed and I let him know this. Immediately, we struck up an agreement for mutual help and co-operation. Then he conducted me inside the broken house for special instruction where he expressed his real motive. Your death is his object but I shall reap no benefit from it. I have committed dark deeds all my life but I have not so far advanced on that sinful path as to cause death of a guileless innocent girl without any ground whatsoever. So I did not fall in with his view. At this moment you came on the spot and, might be, you heard some thing."

"I heard some discussion of that sort."

"That man took me for a fool and offered me some advice. I placed you in hiding in the forest in order to know the trend of the whole thing and give you proper intimation."

"But why did you not come back again?"

"He said many things and so it delayed me to hear his detailed story. You are sure to know him perfectly well. Can you guess who he might be?"

"My former patron, the Kapalik."

"My faith! He it is."

"He gave me a detailed account of how he obtained you on the sea-side—your up-bringing there—Nabokumar's appearance—and your flight with him. Besides, he told me what happened after you had fled with Nabokumar. You don't know what it is all this but I will tell you everything in detail." After this, Luthfunnisha told her every thing—the Kapalik's fall from the hill-top—his fracture of arms—and the dream. Kapalkundala was electrified to hear the dream and a galvinistic shock ran through her heart.

Lutfunnisha continned. "The Kapalik is bent upon carrying out the orders of Bhowani. But, without strength in his arms, he stands in need of a second man's help. He knew me for a Brahmin boy and so he told me everything. I never had been a party to his evil motive though I can not believe my tempestuous mind. I can dare say I shall never agree to his proposal. On the other hand, I shall make every endeavour to thwart his purpose. I proposed this meeting in order to let you know everything, though I have not done this from a selfless pious motive. You must do something for me in return for the life I give you back."

"What can I do for you?" answered Kapalkundada.

"Save me—forsake your husband."

Kapalkundala did not speak for a length of time.

Then, she added "Where shall I go by renouncing my husband?"

"Into an unknown country—far away. I shall give you palace—wealth—servants—and servant-maids and you will spend your days like a princess."

Kapalkundala again set about thinking. Her mind's eye swept all over the wide wide world but could not see any familiar face there. She looked into her heart but, strange! she could not find Nabokumar there. Then why on earth should she be a thorn in the path of Luthfunnisha's happiness?

So she said to Luthfunnisha "I can't realise now whether you have bestowed any benefit upon me. I don't care for your palace—wealth—land—servants and servant-maids. But why should I stand in the way of your happiness? God speed you success! From tomorrow, you shall hear no more of this wrong-doer. A forest-wanderer had I been and a forest-wanderer shall I be."

Luthfunnisha was struck to hear this as she never looked for such a prompt assent. Charmed with the reply, she began "Sister, live long!—you have given me a new life. But I shall never allow you to go away in a helpless condition. Go forth with a trusty clever servant whom I shall send you tomorrow morning. There is a lady friend of mine who holds a high position in Burdwan. She will supply your every want and necessity."

Luthfunuisha and Kapalkundala were so deep in conversation that they could not look there were breakers ahead. Neither of them could see that Nabokumar and the Kapalik, standing by the pathway that ran from the sheltering place, were darting fierce glances at them.

Nabokumar and the Kapalik simply looked on at them as, unfortunately, due to distance, they could not hear a word of the conversation. If men's ears could hear as much as men's eyes can see, who knows whether the load of human misery would have become all the more light or heavy! This earth is God's strange handiwork.

Nabokumar saw that Kapalkundala's untied hair fell across her back in profusion. She used to never braid her hair only when she was on her own. Besides, he saw her mass of hair, sweeping off the back of the Brahmin youth, intermingled with his side-locks. At this, his knees involuntarily bent together and, slowly and gradually, he sat himself down on the earth.

When the Kapalik noticed it, he took out a cocoa-nut shell that was fastened on his girdle and said "My son, you are losing strength. Drink this heroic medicine which is Bhowani's offering as this will restore your strength."

The Kapalik held up the vessel near Nabokumar's lips whereupon he drank off the contents at a draught and thus quenched his thirst. He knew not that the sweet drink was brewed by the Kapalik's own hands and so was a wine of terrible strength. The stimulant gave him power.

On the otherhand, Luthfunnisha softly said to Kapalkundala, "Sister, it is not in my power to requite the good you have done me. But I will think it a happiness if I get a niche in your heart. I have heard the ornaments, I made you a present of, you have given to the poor. I have nothing valuable on my person now. I have brought a ring concealed under the hair of my head with some ulterior object for tomorrow's use. But, God willing, I am spared the ill-use of it. Keep this ring—treat it as a souvenir—and remember your Javan sister afterwards. If husband questions you, today, about this ring tell him you have received it from Luthfunnisha. So saying, Luthfunnisha took out a costly ring from her finger and handed it to Kapalkundala. Nabokumar saw all this and, though under the firm grip of the Kapalik, he trembled from head to foot. The Kapalik gave him another dose of that strong new wine which directly went up to his head. The wine killed all his best instincts and put out the little spark of humanity left in him.

Kapalkundala took leave of Luthfunnisha and went homeward. Subsequently, Nabokumar and the Kapalik followed her along an alley, unobserved by Luthfunnisha.

VIII

HOMEWARD

Slowly and wearily Kapalkundala turned her steps homeward. Slowly and wearily she plodded her way back. The reason was she had been wrapt up in deep thought and meditation. The news of Luthfunnisha wrought a change in the stream of her thoughts. She was ready for self-sacrifice. Self-sacrifice for whom?—for Luthfunnisha?—Oh, No!

Kapalkundala was by nature endowed with a Tantrick's instincts. As the Tantrick always feels remorseless in sacrificing other's lives to earn the good graces of the Kalika, so Kapalkundala was ever ready to lay down her own life for the same purpose. It was not like the Kapalik that her whole existence was treated as a mere abstraction for the attainment of divine favour. But the perception of the practice of piety and devotion to the Divine Energy as manifest in Kalika with her own eyes and ears, by night and day, as well as her habitual religious observances inspired in her a considerable portion of her reverential feelings towards the deity. She conceived the idea of Kali as the ruler of the creation and the bestower of salvation. Imbued with soft tender feelings, she could not bear to see the altar of the goddes dyed red in human blood. But, in no other particulars, would she permit of any breach of observance. That goddess—the ruler of the universe—the dispenser of joys and sorrows—and the giver of final beatitude—now bade her in a dream to sacrifice her own life. Why would she not carry out her behest?

You or I do not court death. We are happy despite what we say to the contrary in a fit of petulance. We move in grooves and spin in this world in quest of happiness and not of sorrow. If ever the consequences of our action defeat our expectations we bawl out life is a misery. Then the conclusion is that sorrow is an exception and not the rule. You and I enjoy happiness and that happiness binds us to the world and makes us loth to leave it. Love is the strongest bond of life. But Kapalkundala had not that binding—in fact she had no binding at all. What else was there, then, to hold her back?

That thing is irresistible in its course which knows no check. When a stream leaps down from the mountain side who is there to stem its flow? Once the air is set in motion who can prevent its blowing. When

BANKIM CHANDRA CHATTERJEE

Kapalkundala lost the equanimity of her mind who would restore its equilibrium? When once the young tusker gets infuriated who can quiet it down?

Kapalkundala questioned her heart "Why should I not consecrate this fleshy body at the feet of the Goddess? What shall I do with this gross mass made up of five elements? She put the question but could not receive any clear reply. Our body has a tie of its own even when life loses all its bindings.

Kapalkundala moved onward, her heart heavy with gloomy thoughts. When human mind is under the sway of some powerful emotion that blots out the sense-perception of the outer world, then preternatural things sometime visualise before the eyes. Such was the case with Kapalkundala.

She seemed to hear a voice from above "My child, let me show the way."

Kapalkundala startled and cast her eyes heavenward. She seemed to see a figure in the sky of the colour of newly-formed clouds. Drops of blood were seen dribbling from the human heads strung round the neck—human hands dangling from the waist—a human skull in the left hand—blood streaming down the body—forehead beaming with an ineffable lustre—and a young moon shining at the corner of the brilliant eyes—as if the goddess Bhairobi was beckoning Kapalkundala by raising her right hand. Kapalkundala proceeded with her face turned upward towards the apparition that were the complexion of new cloulds and sped along the sky in front of her.

That vision set off with a garland of human skulls sometimes hid under clouds and at other times sprang to her eyes.

This was seen neither by Nabokumar nor the Kapalik. Nabokumar under the influence of wine that aroused his passion grew impatient at the slow step of Kapalkundala and broke forth "Kapalik!"

"Anything the matter?" asked the Kapalik.

"Give me more drink" said Nabokumar.

The Kapalik again administered him some wine.

"Is there any more delay?" asked Nabokumar again.

"What is the use of any more delay?" chimed in the Kapalik.

"Kapalkundala" issued the thundering voice of Nabokumar.

Kapalkundala started at the sound. Of late, no body called her by that name. She turned sharply round and stood facing him at which Nabokumar and the Kapalik came before her. She could not recognise, at first, any of them and said "What are you? Are you the messengers of death?"

But the next moment she recognised them and uttered "No,—No! Father. Have you come to sacrifice me?"

Nabokumar caught hold of Kapalkundala with a firm grasp. But the Kapalik in a tender trembling voice said "My child, follow us."

So saying, he led off the party in the direction of the burning ground. Kapalkundala raised her face skyward and looked up where she had seen that frightful form speeding along the sky. Here she saw again that apparition in female form drunk with war-passion and mad for affray, a peal of laughter breaking from her lips, and with along trident directing her on to the pathway followed by the Kapalik. Kapalkundala, as one infatuated by destiny, silently went behind the Kapalik. Nabokumar, as before, held her fast by her hand and went along.

IX

WHERE LAST RITES ARE PAID TO THE DEPARTED HUMANITY

The moon went down leaving the world to darkness. The Kapalik conducted Kapalkundala to the place of worship on a sand-bank bordering on the Ganges. In front of it lay another sand-ridge of a bigger size where stood the burning ground.

Very little water enterd into the deep ravine between the two ridges at flood time so much so that it was left, high and dry, when the stream flowed back. Now there was no water in it. The side of the burning ground facing the Ganges was high and precipitious so that any one trying to land into the river risked a fall into the deep water below. Besides, these sand-banks gradually worn away at the base by the wind-swept waves, breaking against their sides, sometimes, gave way and slipped down into the river depth. There was no light on the place of worship where a little fire was glowing on a piece of wood and the faint glimmer of that light only intensified the horrors of the dimly seen burning ground. Near by, was every arrangement for worship, sacrifice and sacrificial fire. The broad expanse of the Ganges spread out like a vast sheet through the darkness. The summer (Chaitra) wind swept over its breast with violence and the waves, leaping into fury, dashed against the bank, breaking in sheets of spray that leaping down ran past murmering thousand songs. Carrion-beasts of various description sent up their loud wails across the burning ground disturbing the voices of the calm night.

Kapalik made Nabokumar and Kapalkundala sit on mats of sacrificial grass in the appointed places and set about his worship according to Tantrick rites. At the right moment, the Kapalik ordered Nabokumar to fetch Kapalkundala after giving her a dip in the Ganges. So he led Kapalkundala by her hand across the burning ground for a bath. Human bones lying about whitened in the sand pricked into their feet. A pail full of water broke against the feet of Nabokumar and water bursting from it ran down the plane. A dead body lay close by as the wretch had beed denied his last rites. The legs of both as they approached came in contact with it—Kapalkundala went past while Nabokumar trampled it. Carrion-beasts collected round it—some made at them, on their encroachment, while the rest kicked up a noise and fled. Kapalkundala felt Nabokumar's hand tremble on her as she was, herself, without a tinge of fear or tremor.

"Are you afraid?" asked she.

The fumes of wine were gradually working off in Nabokumar's brain and he gravely replied "Afraid, Mrinmonyee?—far from it."

"Why do you tremble, then?"

The question was framed in a voice that can only proceed from a woman's throat—that tone can only issue out from a woman's lips when her heart flows out in tender passions at the sight of other's sufferings. Who knew such a voice would come up the throat of Kapalkundala at the last hour on the burning ground? "Not in fear—I tremble in rage because I can not weep" said Nabokumar.

"Why do you weep?"

The voice had the same tremolo in it.

"Why do I weep?—how would you know it, Mrinmoyee?" returned Nabokumar. "Had you ever upon you the infatuation of the glamour of a charming beauty?"

As he spoke, his voice was stifled with agony.

"Did you ever come to the burning ground" went on he again "to pluck out your heart and fling it into fire?" So saying, he wept aloud and broke down at the feet of Kapalkundala.

"Mrinmoyee—Kapalkundala?—just save me. I roll at your feet—tell me once you are true to your love—tell me that and I will carry you home on my breast."

Kapalkundala raised Nabokumar by his hand and in a soft voice enquired "Why did you not ask me that before?"

The moment, these words were said, they stepped upon the brink of the precipice. Kapalkundala stood in the front with her back upon the river that flowed only one step behind. The tide had set in now and she stood on the top of a sand-mound and spoke "You never asked me that?"

Nabokumar, like a maniac, cried out "I have lost my senses. How could I ask you?—speak—Mrinmoyee!—speak—speak—speak—save me—and let us go home."

"I shall answer what you asked me" said Kapalkundala. "She whom you saw tonight is Padmabati. I never became faithless. What I tell you is a perfect truth. But I shall never return home. I have come to offer my body as sacrifice at the feet of Bhowani—and do it I must. Go home—I must die—and do not weep for me."

"No—Mrinmoyee—No"—exclaimed Nabokumar as he held forth his powerful arms to clasp her to his bosom but he missed her on this side of the grave. A big wave driven by a gust of the summer wind came tumbling on at the foot of the bank where Kapalkundala stood and, struck by it, the top came down with a crash and fell into the river dragging Kapalkundala with it. The noise of the land-slip met the ear of Nabokumar who also saw Kapalkundala disappear under water. Quick as a flash, Nabokumar plunged into the water. He was not a bad swimmer so he swam long and hard in search of Kapalkundala. He could not find her, so he himself never rose.

Tossed, up and down, by a high summer wind that blew across the river, the bodies of Kapalkundala and Nabokumar floated down the stream of the ever-flowing Ganges where who can say?

THE END

A Note About the Author

Bankim Chandra Chatterjee (1838–1894) was an Indian novelist, poet, and journalist. Born into a Bengali Brahmin family, he was highly educated from a young age, graduating from Presidency College, Kolkata with an Arts degree in 1858. He later became one of the first graduates of the University of Calcutta before obtaining a Law degree in 1869. Throughout his academic career, he published numerous poems and stories in weekly newspapers and other publications. His first novel, *Rajmohan's Wife* (1864), is his only work in English. Between 1863 and 1891, he worked for the government of Jessore, eventually reaching the positions of Deputy Magistrate and Deputy Collector. *Anandamath* (1828), a novel based on the Sannyasi Rebellion against British forces, served as powerful inspiration for the emerging Indian nationalist movement. Chatterjee is also known as the author of Vande Mataram, a Bengali and Sanskrit poem set to music by Bengali polymath and Nobel laureate Rabindranath Tagore.

A Note from the Publisher

Spanning many genres, from non-fiction essays to literature classics to children's books and lyric poetry, Mint Edition books showcase the master works of our time in a modern new package. The text is freshly typeset, is clean and easy to read, and features a new note about the author in each volume. Many books also include exclusive new introductory material. Every book boasts a striking new cover, which makes it as appropriate for collecting as it is for gift giving. Mint Edition books are only printed when a reader orders them, so natural resources are not wasted. We're proud that our books are never manufactured in excess and exist only in the exact quantity they need to be read and enjoyed.

bookfinity™

Discover more of your favorite classics with Bookfinity™.

- Track your reading with custom book lists.
- Get great book recommendations for your personalized Reader Type.
- Add reviews for your favorite books.
- AND MUCH MORE!

Visit **bookfinity.com** and take the fun Reader Type quiz to get started.

Enjoy our classic and modern companion pairings!

Classic & Modern

Printed in the USA
CPSIA information can be obtained
at www.ICGtesting.com
JSHW080002150824
68134JS00021B/2241